# BILLIONAIRE'S SINS

L. STEELE

# 1

---

*CLAIM YOUR **FREE** CONTEMPORARY ROMANCE*

*CLAIM YOUR **FREE** PARANORMAL ROMANCE*

*"The fact that I am going to die one day and everyone around me is going to die, and eventually, no one will remember me makes me feel so weird..."*
-From Ava's diary

Ava

"Were you with her when you were married to Mom?"

My father's face pales. Raisa gasps from her seat on the other side of the settee.

"That's not fair, Ava," he admonishes me without raising his voice. "You know I loved your mother."

"And she loved you."

"She'd have wanted me to be happy," he murmurs.

"She wouldn't've wanted you to marry her best friend," I snap. "Not so soon after her death."

"Actually," his lips twist, "this was her idea."

"What?" I blink. "I don't believe it."

"When your mother found out that she was suffering from cancer and had only months to live, she swung into action. She asked Lina to move in with us so we could spend time together, to get comfortable."

"She asked Aunty Lina to move in so she could take care of her," I protest.

"And...so she could ensure that the two of us would give our relationship a chance to work."

"I..." I swallow and my heart begins to drum so hard in my chest that I am sure it's going to burst out of my rib cage. "It's not possible."

My father gives me a sad smile. "Why would I lie to you?"

"Because..." the words choke in my throat, "because you want to paint your relationship in a favorable light with me and Raisa? Because you want us to not hate you for marrying another woman?"

"You're upset about your mother leaving us. You miss her—"

"Don't you?" I frown at him.

"Every single moment of my life. After she died, I wanted to kill myself."

"Dad," I say, shocked.

"It's true." He looks at Raisa, then back at me. "I never wanted to admit it, because what father wants to be seen as weak in front of his children?"

"We aren't kids anymore. We could have handled it if you had shared some of your grief with us. Maybe we could have helped you."

"You were busy trying to get your degree and you—" he turned to Raisa, "you were building your career."

"We'd have made time for you; we'd have found a way," I insist.

"I wouldn't have wanted to take more out of that crucial time in your lives." He shakes his head. "No, your mother was right. She knew I wouldn't be able to go on alone. Even from beyond the grave, that woman made sure I was taken care of. And she chose Lina for it."

"You turned to Lina," I say quietly. "You found comfort in her arms. How long did you wait before Mother was gone before you shagged her?"

"Ava," Raisa snaps, "enough."

"Enough?" I gesture to my father, "Look at him. He doesn't even deny it. Tell me, Dad, how long did you wait after Mum was gone before you turned to her?"

"The truth is, I was in a relationship with Lina before I met your mother."

"What?" Raisa and I exclaim at the same time.

"Then, I met your mother and... I fell headlong in love."

"No." I gape. "This can't be true."

"I loved them both," he holds my gaze, "but I chose your mother."

"And mum knew about your relationship with Lina?"

"They were best friends," he mutters. "They told each other every-thing. Did everything together, those two." His lips quirk, "I always joked there were three of us in that relationship."

His features brighten, and for a few seconds, he seems younger than his fifty-five years. God, he's so young. My mother was only fifty-three, too young to die. They had deserved so much more time together. But apparently, the universe had other plans for both of them. Now, she is in a grave and my father... He is getting ready to marry again. To a woman I've known my entire life. Who'd been with us on so many family holidays. Who was always a welcome guest in our house. I crinkle my eyebrows. Yeah, she'd always been there for us... She'd baby sat us, spent enough time at home to help us with our homework while my mother was busy painting and my father away traveling on work. She'd been here for all my big milestones.

"Oh, my god," I gasp aloud. "That's it."

"What?" Raisa scowls. "What are you thinking?"

I turn to my father, "Lina's always been in love with you too, hasn't she?"

Raisa stares at me. "What are you talking about?"

"Aunty Lina," I snap. "She never got over you. It's why she never married. Why she hung around us all the time. Hell, I bet she was very happy when Mum finally passed so she could finally move in.

Did the two of you have an affair behind her back even before she fell sick? Did you—?"

My father holds up his hand. "Stop," his voice rises, "stop that right now."

"Wow." I shake my head. "Look at you, all defending her now."

"I will not allow you to speak like that of a woman who's wished nothing but the best for us."

"You're not denying it, though. She did carry a torch for you all this time."

My father rubs the back of his neck. "Like I said, we dated. But after I met your mother, it was only her and no one else. I couldn't see myself living my life with anyone but her."

"So, the two of you didn't sleep together while you were married to Mother, before she fell sick?"

Raisa gasps again, "Really, Ava, what's wrong with you?"

"It's fine, Raisa. Best to clear this up right now." My father gazes at me steadily. "I never slept with anyone else except your mother until," he swallows, "until your mother asked me to sleep with Lina."

I gape, "You mean, she asked you two to..."

My father nods, "Your mother wanted us to share a bed while she was alive."

"What?"

My father rises to his feet and walks to the window. He stares out for a few seconds, then turns to me. "She insisted. She did everything in her power to bring us together."

"Oh, and you happily obliged?" My heart begins to race and my pulse pounds at my temples. Adrenaline laces my blood and I jump to my feet. "Mum was on medication, half out of her mind with pain. She likely didn't know what she was asking for—"

"Don't dishonor your mother's memory." He turns on me. "You know she was cogent right until the end. The cancer may have eaten away at her body, but her mind was sharp until the last moment.

I swallow down the tears that threaten. Damnit, my beautiful, proud mother, the glorious woman who had been my role model until the end, the gentle soul who could soothe my fears away with a single word... She had been the most intelligent woman I'd ever known, the most talented artist—who had never had the kind of success she'd deserved. It's why she'd never wanted me to pursue a creative profession, had wanted me to become a doctor. She was the reason that I had tried, until I couldn't keep up the charade. I had left medical school and she had been heartbroken. Sometimes, I wonder if it wasn't the shock of that which had brought on the cancer. *Don't go there. Not now. Not when you're trying to hold it together for the sake of protecting her memory, her legacy. Everything that she had built her entire life.*

"If you expect me to stay quiet just because Mum signed off on this marriage, then you are mistaken." *Shit, what are you saying? You are going to hurt him; you know that.* But I can't stop speaking, can't stop the horrible words from pouring out. "If you marry…that…that woman," I swallow, "I'll… I'll never forgive you, Dad."

My father's gaze intensifies. "You're so adamant, so focused on what only you can see. You're so like her."

The tears I've been keeping down well up and spill from the corners of my eyes. I wipe them away, swallowing down the ball of emotion that clogs my throat. "If I were anything like her, I'd be able to stop you from marrying again, so soon after she's gone."

"It's been six months, Ava," my father says in a low voice. "I'm tired and lonely. You girls have your lives, your careers—"

"One which you still don't approve of, by the way," I mutter.

"Your mother and I wanted the best for you. And it's true, when you said that you couldn't pursue the medical profession, we were shattered. But that's only because we wanted you to have a secure career."

"I have a secure career now." *As a belly dancer, whose dance studio is struggling for funds.* But I don't say that aloud.

"I am proud of you, Ava."

"Are you?"

He nods. "You persisted in your dreams, never backed down. You went after what you wanted and made it happen.

"And me?" Raisa scowls at both of us. "What about me?"

"You're the one I can always rely on to smooth over the cracks in the family."

"Don't do it, Dad." I plead, "Please, just because she asked you to do it, doesn't mean you have to marry Lina. The least you can do is honor her memory by not replacing her in your life."

"I am honoring your mother's memory. By living." He fixes his gaze on me. "Can't you see that?"

"Oh Dad." I bite down on the inside of my cheek, "I know you have a right to be happy, and I want that for you, I do. But replacing Mum..."

"I am not replacing her, Ava." He walks over to me. "No one can. I am simply doing my best to keep going."

"I see." And I do, I really do. It's just, I can't get my head around another woman taking my mother's place in his life. And I don't know if it's better that it's her best friend, or if that makes it worse. "It's just, I need some time to get my head around that. Is that okay?"

He peers into my eyes, then nods. "Okay." His lips quirk. "Okay, Ava."

I turn to leave and Dad calls out, "Wait. You'll come to the wedding, won't you?"

"I... I am not sure," I say without turning around. Then I walk out the door.

# 2

*Two days later*

*"Each blossom still blooms in its field; each child still clutches your hand; each friend still lingers in your heart. And that...is where time goes."*

I glance at the words I've scrawled out in my diary.

My heart stutters. The hair on my forearms rises. Time. Why am I so obsessed with time? I am only nineteen; I have my entire life in front of me. So why do I often ponder how fast time goes by? How it can all be over in a matter of minutes... Blink, and it's gone. A mother playing with her son as an infant one second; the next, he's all grown up and she's shooting a movie with him as her subject. The son, who is the mirror image of her first and only love, the man she fell for, her soulmate...who turned out not to be. And now she has him... The son, who is the image of the father. *Stop it...* All these thoughts that meld and flow and turn my brain to mush. Even *Twilight* was more cheerful than this.

I hear a splash from the pool, and glance around from my perch on the chair in the far corner of the pool area. I am at my friend Summer's townhouse in Primrose Hill. It's February and freezing in London. Which is why I had grabbed my book and my blanket, then crawled over to the far end of the pool area. I'd hidden behind the wide trunk of the oak-tree, then settled down to write.

People hate the cold. Me? I thrive on it. Darkness is my friend, my companion. It clothes me, hides me from the sight of the world, like this blanket that I've wrapped around myself. If I look down, I can see the slope of Primrose Hill fall away below, the grass an undulating carpet that stretches down to the canal. This early in the day, it is quiet, except for a few joggers... And the man who'd dived into the pool and is now swimming laps.

From my hiding place, I can see his massive shoulders flex as he cuts through the water. He propels forward, leaving ripples in his wake. He's moving so fast, he's almost a blur as his powerful arms slice through the water. He hits one end of the swimming pool, then pushes away and begins to swim toward the other side. He zips forward, flings out an arm, thrusts the other back so his body shoots ahead. He lunges onward, keeps going until he hits the other edge of the pool, then turns back. I watch as he does five more laps of the pool... Hell, is he training for a triathlon or something? My entire body hurts, thinking of the punishment he's putting himself through. What the hell is he trying to prove anyway?

He hits the edge of the pool, throws his arms over the rim and holds on. Then he presses his hands down on the ground, hauls himself up. He pitches his leg up and over. The corded muscles of his thigh tauten as he raises himself up and over the side. Water streams down from his sculpted chest, the cut planes of his back, and pours down the sides of his thighs. He raises his arms, throws back his head and stretches. For a second, he stands poised. The first rays of the sun hit his skin, and he seems to sparkle. My throat dries. All of my nerve endings pop. Moisture pools in my core. A shiver runs down my spine.

He turns, giving me a full-frontal view and I draw in a breath. I saw him at my friend Karina's wedding, a few weeks ago. Only difference, he had more clothes on...and he wasn't this wet. *Nor was I—ha!* Nor did he have his thick hair slicked back to outline the contours of his scalp. Nor did the hollows under his cheekbones seem this prominent. I trace my gaze down his hooked nose to his thin upper lip, made all the more pronounced by his full lower lip, which seems soft, pouty enough for me to sink my teeth into and suck. My belly clenches. My core softens. I squeeze my thighs together, watch as he moves toward the deckchair and picks up a towel. He drags it down his massive chest, across that ripped stomach, down the crotch of his black swimsuit, which outline what he's packing. I bite down on the inside of my cheek. Is that man packing or what?

Is he some kind of athlete? He has that strength and confidence that comes with someone who works a physical profession. Or else, he trains a lot. As evidenced by this morning's work out.

He loops the towel around his neck, straightens, then meets my gaze.

I pull back. "Shit, shit, shit." *Did he see me? Of course, he spotted me.* He seems like the kind of man who wouldn't miss a thing in his surroundings.

Go on, get out there and wave at him or something. Tell him 'Hi.'

"Hi." I wiggle my fingers in the air in his general direction, too embarrassed to look that way again.

"Hello, there." A gruff voice sounds above me and I yelp. My heart pounds in my chest as I glance up, straight at eye-level with his gorgeous crotch—now covered by his pants. He'd managed to pull those on before heading over, apparently. Not that it does anything to hide, but rather, reveals the gargantuan proportions of whatever it is that it encloses.

*Jeez, get your mind out of the gutter, bitch.*

I raise my gaze, and hell, if the view doesn't get even more serious. Dense muscles, packed one on top of the other, moving, slipping, sliding as he draws in a breath. An intricate design inches over one shoulder, and damn, if I don't want to jump up and peek around to find out how it continues across his back.

He folds his arms across his chest and his biceps bulge.

Heat sears my blood. My thighs clench.

I tilt my head back, and further back. The sun chooses that moment to shine on him again, shadowing his features. This guy is a sun trap; that's for sure. The golden glow folds about him, caresses him, so sparks of amber flare in the air around him. I blink, and his face comes into view. Dark close-cropped hair slicked back from the water. His eyes are golden...amber with a hint of black in their depths. Like he has secrets which he holds close to his chest. Thick eyelashes that sweep down over high cheekbones you could cut yourself on. I curl my fingers into fists and my nails dig into my flesh.

A scar mars the expanse of his left cheek, and somehow that only heightens how perfect the rest of his face is.

"You okay?" He tilts his head.

"Of course." My voice cracks and I clear my throat. "Why wouldn't I be?"

"You seem like you saw something...unexpected?"

"Uh, you're not a vampire, are you?"

He blinks, then chuckles. A full-throated, deep reverberation that sucker-punches me in the gut. My thighs tremble. My toes curl. I watch as those full lips of his quirk.

"I'm Edward." He holds out his hand.

"Wha—" I gape, "you're kidding me, right?"

He frowns. "Excuse me?"

"Your...your name," I choke out. "It can't be Edward."

"I am not following..." His cultured tone carries a note of warning, which I ignore.

"I mean, you can't be called Edward. Who put you up to this? Was it Isla?" Only she knows about my slightly stalkerish obsession with Edward, from Twilight, and surely, she wouldn't tell the others, right?

"Ah." The wrinkles on his forehead dissipate. "You're Isla's friend?"

I hold out my hand, "Ava."

"Ava?" He frowns.

He touches my hand and the rest of the words dry in my throat. Goosebumps flare on my skin. His gaze widens and the planes of his chest twitch. Did he feel that shock of the impact as well? I try to pull back my hand but he holds onto it.

"Why are you hiding, Eve?"

"I'm not," I scowl. "and that's not my name."

"It suits you better," he tilts his head, "and you haven't answered my question yet."

"Which one?"

"What are you doing here?"

"I came here to write," I bite the inside of my cheek, "only... I heard the splashing in the pool and I turned around and spotted you swimming.

"And you watched?" His lips curl in a hint of a smirk.

I glance away. "I, uh, may have peeked a bit."

"Did you like what you saw?"

I jerk my head in his direction, to find him watching me closely. His expression is one of curiosity, like I am some kind of lab specimen whose responses he is clocking in a clinical way. The hair on the back of my neck rises. I want to glance away, break the connection with this man, but I can't. My pulse rate ratchets up. Despite the chill in the morning, my palms begin to sweat. I clear my gaze, force the words out, "Wh....why Eve?"

"You know why." He peruses my features. "And you haven't answered the question."

"Do I?" My heart begins to race. "And what question?"

"You know the answer to both." He folds his arms across his chest and his impressive biceps bulge. Heat blooms between my legs and I resist the urge to rub my thighs together.

"I'm not sure what you're referring to," I say stiffly, "and no, I don't find you attractive."

His grin widens, and the impact of that smile... Oh, my. His teeth sparkle against the tan of his skin, his features brighten, the charisma pours off of him, and honestly, I can't glance away. I take in the gleam in his eyes, the hair on his forehand drying and already curling a little.

I blink. "Aren't you cold?"

The breeze picks up, and a strand of hair whips across my face.

He releases my hand, only to lean down and push the hair aside.

Goosebumps pop on my skin. My stomach trembles and my heart begins to race. I watch as his gaze holds mine, as the pupils of his eyes dilate. His nostrils flare, and he straightens. "I'd better be going. Sinclair's expecting me for breakfast."

"Oh, that's right. Me too." I'd promised Summer I'd join them for breakfast. I jump up, and the movement brings me close to him. The heat of his body slams into my chest and my throat dries. I stare up at him, as he glares down his nose. Something like anger steals across his features, before he schools all expression from his face. A strange sensation grips my chest. I draw in a breath and the oxygen rushes to my head. Shit, when had I forgotten to breathe? He steps back, and the cold air rushes in. I shiver.

He pivots, walking toward the pool house. I take in the tattoo of the snake that crawls diagonally across his back. Whoa! That's one mean-ass tattoo. It's as spectacular as it is unexpected against the much paler skin of his back. The forked tongue of the snake is thick in girth, and within it are etched tribal signs that I can't decipher. The edge of it flows over his shoulder, which is what I must have seen earlier. The scales on the snake are patterned in color and the triangular head has slitted eyes which seem to follow me as I jump to my feet, then tug the blanket around me, hold my book close and follow.

"Hold on," I protest, "your legs are too long."

He slows his pace and I catch up.

"So, you are a friend of Sinclair's?"

He nods.

"You're one of the Seven, aren't you?" I peer up into his face, "I saw you at Arpad and Karina's wedding."

His jaw hardens. Now what did I say for him to seem angry?

"Surely, you remember?" I mutter. "Didn't you notice me?"

"I don't notice every girl who crosses my path."

I blink, then pause my steps, "Now, that's not fair. I could have sworn that you saw me there. Besides, I am not a girl."

He pulls forward, and I run to catch up. "Did you hear what I said?" I demand. "I am not a—"

"Girl." He stops so quickly that I bump into him. The scent of chlorine, and under that, the fresh-cut grass scent of him teases my nostrils. I draw in a breath, filling my lungs with his earthy essence. Moisture pools in my center and my nerve-endings seem to fire all at once. Why the hell does he have to smell so utterly delectable?

He pivots to face me and the heat of his body seems to turn up a notch. Does this man have a furnace under his skin, or what?

He looks me up and down. "What are you then?" he asks.

"What—" I blink.

"You said you are not a girl, so what are you?"

I tip up my chin. "A woman." I square my shoulders. "I am a woman."

"And I..." He squares his shoulders, "I am sworn to celibacy."

# 3

Edward

"Excuse me?" She gapes. "What...what did you say?"

*Shit, what the hell had I been thinking? Why had I blurted that out?* Because I am attracted to her... There, the simple truth. I've never been so affected by a woman as I have been since I first saw her at City Hall when she'd appeared next to the bride...and my world had reduced, shrunk down to her eyes, her mouth... That aura of her which shines so brightly, so purely. So innocent. How old is she anyway?

How could I have known then, that she would be trouble? That every single thing I'd sworn off, every vow I had taken... All of it would culminate in this test. This...trial that God has selected for me. And I cannot give in. No way. Not by all that I hold dear to me. There is space for only one attraction, one relationship, one complete obsession. To the One Above.

So, I had taken the easy way out. The cowardly way, you say?

Maybe, but it is better to be upfront about what I am. I need to be clear that there can never be anything between us...

Hell, why am I even thinking along those lines? Not that she seems unduly affected by me, but that spark of awareness between us... I hadn't imagined that. Or the way her pupils had dilated, or how she had leaned in to me, how she'd sniffed me. She says she's not a girl anymore... but I beg to differ. She's all female, all coltish limbs and a translucent skin that reflects whatever she is feeling.

"I have taken a vow." I step back from her. "I have promised to live a celibate life. I have completely given my life to Christ and the people I have been called to serve."

I turn away from her, head for the clothes that I'd placed on the pool-chair.

The hair on the nape of my neck prickles.

I glance over my shoulder to find her staring at me. Her gaze runs down my back, then back to my face, as I snatch up my shirt and shrug into it.

"I... I don't understand."

"Me neither." I grab my towel, then head for the guesthouse that I occupy whenever I stay over at the Sterlings', which isn't often. But when I'd wanted to leave yesterday, the rest of the Seven wouldn't hear of it. With Arpad getting married, it means all of us are now hitched... Well, except me... And Baron. I stiffen. *Why the hell am I thinking of him?* The friend who'd turned his back on us and left. Not that he hasn't been in touch. He's communicated through snail mail, writing on occasion, like when Damian was hesitant about getting married to Julia. Or when there is a specific investment that Sinner or Saint aren't sure about, though how he knows this is beyond me. The two of them run 7A Investments, one of the leading financial services firms in the country. Between them, they've managed to invest our money such that we'll be living off the wealth created for this entire lifetime. Not that I am going to touch a penny of it.

My investments go toward FOK Media, aka Full of Kindness Media, the non-profit that the Seven set up to finance upcoming talent in return for a portion of their earnings. I'd also put money toward my own trust that supports the most vulnerable and those in need.

As for myself, I stay in a small two-bedroom home, owned by the parish I am devoted to serving. The place where I need to return before things get further out of hand. It had been wrong to approach her in the first place. I'd seen her watching me, had recognized her— Of course, I had. I couldn't have missed her—and then I had approached her. I should have walked away, but I couldn't resist. I had to see her once more. And now I have to atone for the sinful thoughts I entertained.

I clench my fists at my sides.

"Wait." Her footsteps approach me, and I increase my pace.

I cannot be alone with her, not for one more second.

"What are you trying to tell me, Edward?"

I reach the guesthouse, twist open the door and step in. I turn to find her hesitating at the entrance and beckon her in.

She hesitates and I tilt my head. "Come on, I have something to show you."

"You do?" Her forehead furrows.

"You need to see this."

She blows out a breath and follows me. I head inside, to the bedroom, take my collar from where I'd placed it on the bedstead. I slip it on, then turn to find her poised at the doorway.

Her face pales; her jaw drops.

"You're a...a—"

"Priest." I nod.

"B...but," she opens and shuts her mouth, "you weren't wearing a collar at the wedding yesterday."

"I'm a diocesan priest. I wear the collar when I have anything pastoral to do. I don't usually wear it when out with friends."

"I see." She shrugs off her blanket, folds it over her arm. Her gaze skitters away. "I knew it was too good to be true. Of course, it is." She retreats into the living room, drops the blanket and her book on the couch and begins to pace. "I mean, just once, things couldn't be easy for me, right? Everything has to be complicated. Just this once, couldn't things have worked out the way they do for everyone else? Of course, not." She throws up her hands. "This is not fair, not fair at all."

"Are you..." I follow her as she stomps back-forth-back, across the length of the floor of the living room. "Are you talking to yourself?"

"Shh." She turns to me and frowns. "I'm trying to figure this out."

"By talking aloud?"

"Hey, don't mock it until you try it. Did you know talking to yourself helps you organize your thoughts?" She shoves her purple-tipped hair back from her face.

Who dyes their hair purple? Ava does, that's who.

"According to psychologists, talking out loud to yourself helps you clarify your thoughts," she mumbles. "It helps to figure out what's important, and firm up any decisions you're contemplating."

"Ah," I allow my lips to tip up, "and what decision are you contemplating right now?"

She flushes. "I am not sure you want to know."

"Don't I?"

She shakes her head. "I don't think it's right for me to share what I am thinking with a priest... Not unless I was in confession, but then, wouldn't you have to keep it secret? I mean, aren't you bound by a code of conduct of some kind? And damn, but I admit, I may have eyed you up a little out there earlier. Does that even count as sin? Is it made worse by the fact that you are priest? Is it—"

"Stop." I hold up my hand.

She purses her lips together, then draws in a breath. "Sorry," she mutters, "I tend to babble when I'm nervous."

"I didn't notice." I allow my smile to widen. This girl—she's adorable. She twists her fingers together, hunches her shoulders, then snaps them back. "Uh, guess I should...go then?"

She turns to leave, and something hot stabs at my chest. Okay, so I can't have any kind of relationship with her... What the—? How had I even allowed myself to think that? Since becoming an ordained priest eight years ago, I've focused on my role, the routine, the discipline. The simplicity of my existence means everything to me. It helps me ground my thoughts, allows me to focus on what is important: serving others, helping them, listening to them, and helping to alleviate their worries.

In their comfort, I draw comfort. By easing their pain, I breathe easier. When I help a soul cross over, a part of me opens up to possibilities, and when I baptize a newborn, look into their clear eyes and welcome them to the house of the Lord, I redeem myself.

That... The regiment of how I live my life, gives me the framework upon which to anchor myself. When I am in that space, I don't have to worry about what happened to me, how the incident affected me, how I had fallen apart after the kidnapping, when the Seven and I had been taken and held in captivity for a month; how I had pulled myself together, only to fall apart again.

Boys join the army to learn discipline... For me, it had been the calling from God that had saved me. And surely, it is God who sent this girl, this absolutely stunning, untainted-by-life soul to me.

*Or is it the devil trying to lure me away from Him?*

No, not possible. I shake my head. This... It doesn't feel wrong. There's nothing unnatural about what I feel for her. Surely, it has to be the Lord wanting me to learn something from her? That's why he sent her.

What is this test that I am facing? And do I have the courage to go through with it?

Can I rise to the occasion; face the fears that her proximity evokes in me?

And if I don't—if I chose *not* to accept this ultimate trial... Would that not mean that I have learned nothing from all the time I have spent in serving the Lord?

If this is his way of testing me... And surely, it has to be. There could be no other explanation for why, out of everything I've encountered thus far, she stands out like a beacon...

The air around her crackles with a vitality, a strange sensation... Almost one of hope, of life, of joy... Emotions I've seen amongst my parishioners, that I have studied from afar, even joined them in celebrating... But never once, experienced personally. Not until now.

*Is this why you sent her my way, my Lord? Is it a sign that I need to open myself further, allow the emotions in, sense their sting, revel in how they torture me with everything that I cannot and will not allow myself to feel? So be it, then. I follow your command.*

"Ava," I call out as she opens the door, "wait."

# 4

Ava

His voice stops me. I pause at the threshold.

"Ava."

I turn, wait for him to speak.

"I ..." He shoves his hands inside his pockets. "I'm sorry," he finally says.

"For what?"

"For giving you the wrong impression earlier." He stares at me. "Perhaps some of the fault is with me too."

"Oh?" I stare. Is he going to apologize to me? Why? Because I was drawn to him? *Please, don't... Please, please, don't.* My cheeks heat, and I glance away, "I mean, seriously, it was nothing." I hold my blanket in front of me. Can I hide under it, maybe? No, that would only look silly... As if anything could be worse than our earlier encounter? Gosh, how could I have been attracted to him? He's a priest... Someone sworn to not sleep with anyone, and I can't stop staring at his perfect features. Those high cheekbones, his dark hair cut short at the sides, long on top, that hooked nose, the mean upper lip...that gorgeous throat I want to lick, the width of his shoulders that fills the doorway, cutting out the sight of the room behind him. He draws in a breath and the sculpted planes of his chest stretch the fabric of his shirt. Not that I am staring or anything. Of course, not.

I clear my throat, then glance away.

"I should be the one apologizing." I clutch at my blanket with palms that are slippery with sweat. *Dear God... What's wrong with me? And by the way, I need to have words with You. It's not fair that You dangle someone as luscious as this man in front of me only to claim him and tell me that I can't have him.* OMFG. I am seriously losing it, if I am having conversations with the Power Above in my head. "I shouldn't have sneaked looking at you earlier, and well... It's just, you're so damn gorgeous to look at, and well, I couldn't help it."

"Did you just tell me that I'm gorgeous to look at?'

I glance up to find him staring at me with surprise and bemusement.

"Yes," I shuffle my feet, "I guess I did."

"Do you always say everything that comes into your head?"

"Kind of," I hunch my shoulder, "though honestly, I seem to have even less of a filter when you're around."

"Do I make you nervous?" One corner of his lip curls...just a tad. Holy hell, he smirked. No, he totally did. And damn, if that isn't the hottest thing I have seen. Right after the Edward I'd read about in Twilight and imagined myself as Bella.

And here I am as Ava, and this is my Edward right here. Except, this scenario is all wrong. Shit. I'm tying myself in knots. I stare at him. "Are you sure you're a priest?"

He chuckles, "The last time I checked." He glances down at me, something like amusement and regret lacing his features. "Are you a...?" He tilts his head, "What do you do, Ava?"

"I'm a, uh, dancer."

"A dancer?" He frowns.

"Not ballet," I add quickly because that's what most people assume automatically, "more like, the exotic kind."

"Exotic kind?"

"A belly dancer." I twitch my hips, more out of habit than anything else. Okay, so maybe not completely... Maybe it's to take in how his nostrils flare as he lowers his gaze to my hips and stays there, as if fascinated by what he sees.

"A belly dancer, huh?" He finally raises his gaze to meet mine and those gorgeous golden-brown eyes of his blaze at me. Then he lowers his eye lashes, and when he raises them, all emotion is shorn from his features.

"I, uh, dropped out of university. I'd joined to study medicine, but somehow...half-way through my first year, I lost interest. Turns out, becoming a doctor requires a strong stomach. The first time I saw a cadaver, I fainted and then had nightmares for days. I couldn't enter the laboratory after that. Also, the smell of formaldehyde—the solution they use to preserve specimens? Turns out, I am allergic to it... So..."

I swallow.

"Shit. Uh... Shoot, I am sorry. I'm blabbing." I shuffle my feet. "All that untapped energy, you know, it needs an outlet. It's why I turned to dancing, and then started my own studio teaching belly dancing. It makes me happy, you know—dancing?" *Stop it, what the hell are you doing? Pouring out your thoughts in a stream of consciousness?* "In fact, my dream is to one day to have a home big enough to have a studio in it so whenever I want to dance, I'll have my own space. A place where I can just be myself... You know?" I bite the inside of my cheek. So much for trying to appear calm and composed. OMG, what's wrong with me? I wipe my clammy palms against the fabric of my dress.

"So, I make you nervous?" He quirks an eyebrow, curls his fists at his sides, and whoa, his knuckles are white. I tilt my head, take in the nerve that throbs at his temple, the way his chest rises and falls. Maybe... I'm not the only one affected. Maybe, he feels it too—the connection, this strange chemistry between us that's crackled since his gaze met mine. Only... It means nothing. It can't... He's a priest...and I? I'm a hot mess.

"You do." I step back. "You make me very unsure of myself, Ed—" I bite down on the inside of my cheek. Should I call him Edward? Father? Damn, this is not cool, not at all. "I really should go."

He lowers his chin, "Guess I'll see you for breakfast at the main house then?"

"Breakfast?"

"You are going to eat breakfast with Sinclair and Summer, I assume?"

"Ah," I swallow, "yes, of course."

He nods, then holds out his hand, "It's nice to meet you, Ava."

Nice? Okay, not the word I would have used, but if he wants to play it that way, well, so can I.

I tilt my head, "And you, Father."

His jaw tics. A mask seems to form from his features as he draws himself up to his full height. He's so tall that I have to tip my head all the way back to see his face. How can someone so big, so vital, someone whose every inch of his body is packed with sex appeal... How the hell could he have dedicated himself to a life where he'll never experience pleasures the likes of which I want to share with him?

And then, there's his personality... The intensity of his gaze, the depth I sense underneath that tightly controlled exterior. The strength of his dominance that he wears about himself, tightly cloaked, held back, as if he doesn't dare give in to the power of his complete self... because it would be too much for everyone around him. For the man he is, and make no mistake, he is one-hundred percent alpha male, would outshine anyone around him. Is that the depth of his sacrifice? The depth of what he'd given up to pursue his calling?

He holds my gaze, then nods. "Goodbye, Ava."

I clutch my blanket and book to my chest, then turn and head toward the main house. The hair on the nape of my neck rises and I know he's watching me as I put distance between us. My stomach clenches; my guts twist. *Don't look back. Don't.* My heart begins to hammer in my chest. This is just silly. Why the hell do I feel like I'm leaving a part of myself behind? I pause, glancing over my shoulder to find he's still there in the doorway. Our gazes connect; a thrill runs up my spine. My pores pop. Even across that distance I can make out the tension that coils those massive shoulders, those cut abs of his that are outlined by the fabric of the shirt he wears, the trim waist, the powerful thighs clad in pants that cling to his every groove, every ridge, every muscle that cords his legs.

I gulp. My throat closes. All the moisture in my body drains to my core. *No, no, no, you can't think of him that way, remember.* I avert my gaze, turn and half-run until I reach the main house. I let myself inside, then race up the stairs. I reach the landing of the first floor, and bump into someone.

"Hey, where's the fire?" Isla, one of my closest friends, asks.

*It's inside me, all around me,* is what I want to stay. I firm my lips, peer up into her face.

"You, okay?" she asks. "You look like you've seen a ghost.

No, just a man I want... Who is the last man on this earth I can have. Shit, why can't my life be more like one of those romance novels I love to read? Where the only thing standing between me and the hero is a string of inconsequential misunderstandings?

"Ava?" Isla touches my shoulders. "Say something."

"Something," I mutter.

She chuckles, "You want some coffee?" She grips my hand. "You seem chilled."

"I am," I admit, "I was out, uh, writing in my journal."

"You went out dressed like that?" She stares at my dress. "You didn't wear a jacket?"

"I had this." I nod to the blanket.

"You still seem frozen."

Maybe that's because of the surprise I just had? A cold sensation invades me. Shit, how could he be a priest? Seriously, a man who looks like that, who's vital, and hot and so sexy. How had he renounced the world? Or maybe, only monks do that. I have no idea what it means to devote oneself to the service of the church. How could I? My parents had been agnostic. I've never been drawn to any religion.

Then my mother had passed away and I'd been convinced that there definitely isn't a God. If there were, why had he taken my mother away from me?

"Ava?" Isla tugs on my arm, "Come on, let's get some coffee and breakfast, and you can tell me all about your adventures this morning."

"What adventures?" I frown, but allow her to lead me back the way I came. We walk into the large kitchen that looks out on the backyard—correction— that looks out on the entire freakin' slope of Primrose Hill. The money has its benefits, no doubt, but surely, too much of it can't be healthy. It blinds you to the real stuff—feelings, emotions, relationships... Hell, the only thing I know about myself is that I want to live as close to my true self as possible. Which means identifying what I want for myself in the first place.

She places two cups on the counter, then scoops coffee into the cafetière, before switching on the kettle to boil the water.

"The adventures that have put that dazed look on your face." She stabs a finger in my direction, "Fess up. Did you crawl out to meet someone?"

"What?" I blink, "No."

"You can tell me." She waggles her eyebrows. "You have a boyfriend hidden away you don't want the rest of us to meet?"

"Nothing like that." The kettle switches off, she turns, pours water over the coffee grounds, then stirs it, before lowering the plunger.

The scent of coffee wafts around me and I blink as if coming out of a mirage. I place my blanket and book on the island as she pours out the coffee, then offers me a mug. I top it up with cream and three spoonfuls of sugar, then take a sip.

"So," she asks, "what happened to send you tearing through the corridor like you were trying to get away from a shark."

"Do you believe in fate?" I query.

She blinks, then blows on the liquid in her mug. She takes a sip, sighs, then leads the way to one of the barstools.

I slip onto the one next to her, place my mug on the counter. "Well?" I ask. "Do you?"

"Of course." She gazes into the depths of the dark liquid in her mug. "And being as how so many of the Seven have found their match... When honestly, it's hard to believe any of them would ever end up together with someone else, based on the journeys that each of them has gone through..." She rubs her cheek. "It has to be fate...or destiny, or whatever you want to call it, guiding them to get together."

"But what if fate gives you mixed signals?" I rub my hand across my face.

"Mixed signals?"

I nod, "You know, like telling you to move forward yet holding you back, for some reason."

"I don't understand." She scowls. "Are you telling me you met someone, and you are sure you were destined to meet him, only now you think he can't be the one for you?"

"Kind of." I twist my fingers together. "It's more like, I shouldn't have been attracted to him in the first place, because he's unavailable."

"He's married?"

"No." I shake my head. "Kind of. He's in a relationship with someone else."

She gives me a hard look. "So, he's involved with someone else, and yet, he encouraged you?"

"Not knowingly." I wriggle around to find a more comfortable stance. "I mean, he didn't do anything to encourage me. It was me, making assumptions about him."

"But he told you he is with someone else?"

"That's the thing. He's not with someone else."

"So, he's available?" She frowns.

"No." I hunch my shoulders.

"So," she purses her lips, "he's not with someone else, but he's not available?"

I jut out my lower lip.

"What, is he a priest or something?" She chuckles.

I stare at her and my cheeks flame.

"Omigod." She opens and shuts her mouth, "No way, don't tell me."

I bury my head in my hands, "Oh…this is soooo embarrassing."

"Don't tell me." She grips my arm. "You're talking about Edward, aren't you?"

I nod, still not meeting her eyes. Jeez, does everyone know that he's a priest? How had I missed that memo? But then, I hadn't spent any time with the Seven. I'd seen Edward at Karina and Arpad's wedding, but he hadn't been wearing his priest's collar, so I could be forgiven for making that mistake, right?

"So, you had no idea he was a priest?" Her voice is filled with sympathy.

"I must be the only one who didn't know." I lower my hands, raise my gaze to hers. "I mean, look at the guy… He's…so hot, has so much presence. He's a walking orgasm, for hell's sake."

"Who's a walking orgasm?" Summer ambles over to us. She plucks the cup of coffee in front of me on the counter and takes a long satisfying sip. "Mmmm." She swallows, then glances between us, "So who were you talking about?"

"Edward," Isla blurts out, before I have a chance to tell her to shut up.

I glare at her and she raises her shoulders.

"The hot priest?" Summer places the cup of java back on the counter top, then walks over to a shelf near the refrigerator. She pulls out two boxes of cereal, pivots and takes a seat at the island. "Can't talk about sexual frustration without sugar."

She slides the box of Froot Loops to me, then dips into the box of Cinnamon Toast Crunch. Crunching down a mouthful, she leans forward, "So give."

I push away the cereal, pick up my cup of coffee. "Nothing to give."

"She's attracted to Edward," Isla adds.

"Argh," I groan, "now I feel like a fool."

"Because he's a priest?" Summer tilts her head.

"Umm, yeah?" I bury my nose in my cup. "Surely, it must be blasphemy or something to entertain thoughts of the sexual kind about a man dedicated to the Church?"

"I don't blame you." Summer's lips kick up at the corners. "That man makes me wanna go back to church."

"I bet there's a line of women lining up to go to mass when he preaches." Isla chuckles.

"I'm first in line for communion." Summer nods.

"You'll have to battle it out with me." Isla snorts.

"I'll simply get in line twice." Summer laughs.

"I'll be an altar server with nothing under my robes," Isla retorts.

"Wait... what?" My cheeks heat. "What the hell are you two going on about. Seriously?" I scowl at Isla. "Don't talk about him that way, okay?"

"Ooh." Isla bats her eyelids. "Woman's already getting possessive."

"I am not getting possessive." I grit my teeth. "I am simply stating that it's wrong to talk about a priest in those terms."

"Oh, dear." Isla blinks. "Oh, dear."

"What?" I frown.

"Oh, dear, oh, dear, oh, dear." Isla shakes her head.

"What, what?" I stare at her. "What the hell is wrong with you? Why do you suddenly sound like someone from a Jane Austen novel?"

"Because you're acting like one of the shy women who often appears in her stories?"

"I am not shy, and Jane Austen's women were feisty heroines who could hold their own." I hunch my shoulders. " Also, it's not all physical with him, okay? There's something else going on here... Something I can't put a finger on."

"You sense a connection with him," Summer scoops up more of her cereal. "And I'd be the first to say that's not something you should dismiss."

"What do you mean?"

"How many men do you think you are going to meet in life with whom you have that kind of instant link?"

"I don't know."

"Not many," she replies. "So, when you sense that kind of bond, you don't let it go. Only—"

"Only he's a priest?"

"There is that. And it's Edward we're talking about here. Everything I've heard about him from Sin, confirms to me that he's focused on the Church and his path. I've heard the rest of the Seven talk about how he'd never turn from it."

"Shit." I squeeze my eyes shut. I knew it. I mean, of course, I did. After all, I am attracted to him. And what I know about him, so far, has confirmed to me that he doesn't do anything by half measures. He is dedicated to the Church. No way, is he going to walk away. In fact, I shouldn't even be thinking about him in this fashion.

Summer grips my shoulder and I snap open my eyes.

"So, what are you going to do about it?" Her forehead is furrowed.

"What can I do?" I slink down further into my seat, "He's a priest, end of..."

"Is it?" Isla frowns. "Do you actually believe that?"

"Yes...No." I slide off the stool and begin to pace. "I don't know. I mean, a part of me wants to walk away. The other part insists that there's a reason that he's called Edward, right?"

There's silence, then the two of them look at each other. "You're talking about *Twilight*?" Isla leans back in her seat. "Tell me you're not... Not that I don't have a thing for Edward."

I shoot her a dirty look, and she holds up her hands. "I meant the character, not your Edward."

"He's not my Edward." I fold my arms about my waist. "And he probably never will be." I turn on them, "But...the fact that he's named after my favorite character ever; that has to be the only reason I am so strongly attracted to him... Right? And yet... There's this barrier between us, one which can't be overcome."

"Why can't it be overcome?" Isla scowls, "I know he's a priest, but men have given up a lot more for true love."

*True love. Is it love? Or just lust?* I wrap my arms about my waist, "I only just met the man."

"I wish I could tell you to walk away, but when you feel that connection," Summer thumps her chest, "it's not something you can easily ignore."

"What would you have me do?" I lean a hip against the island. "It's not like the challenge is easy to surmount." *Although I'd certainly like to try to mount him*, I think with a smirk.

"It never is," Isla retorts.

"I know... I know, but this situation... It's crazy. I mean, am I supposed to seduce him away from his calling?"

"Maybe," Isla concedes, "maybe not."

"What do you mean?"

"I understand your reticence in not doing anything to sway him from his path... It takes a special kind of person to follow his calling," she says slowly.

"That's what I mean. Who am I to stand between him...and... his..." I bite the inside of my cheek, "his loyalty, his devotion to the path he's decided on? I just met him... Hell, I don't even know how he feels about me...except..."

"Except?" Isla prompts me.

"He did apologize to me, in case he'd given me the wrong impression."

"Ah," Summer cups her chin in her hand, "so he's aware of the chemistry between the two of you."

I wince, "Should we even be using adjectives like chemistry? Somehow, it seems so wrong, given the context, you know?"

Isla pushes back from the table. "Woman, you are making my head ache, the way you are over analyzing this. I think you are putting too much emphasis on the fact that he's called Edward. Not that I have anything against the story, but this is real life, and it doesn't always follow a predictable storyline, know what I mean?"

"You're telling me?" I snort. "So what? I should ignore it completely?"

"Or just give it time, let it breathe, see how things develop," Isla offers. "Maybe the attraction will fizzle out—?"

Umm, I don't think so, but okay, I am willing to wait and see.

"Maybe he'll decide you're worth it?" Summer points out. "If his feelings develop further, maybe he'll do something about it?"

"Is that what you told Karma as well?" Karma, Summer's sister has been holed up in Sicily with her new hottie and Summer hasn't heard from her in a few months, except for text messages.

Summer's brow furrows, "I never did get a chance to share that advice with Karma. She just up and left one day, which is out of character for her. And I confess, I am worried about what she's up to, but each time I tell her that I am coming to Sicily to hunt her down, she insists that it won't be long before she returns."

"Has she kept in touch with you?"

"We text every weekend. Every time I message her, she replies instantly." Summer chews on her lower lip.

"But you are still worried about her?"

"I am, and yet," Summer hesitates, "I don't want to stifle her, you know? I trust my sister, and while I want to protect her, I also know that we have to make our own mistakes to learn from them too."

"Mistakes," I muse. "Wonder if I am mistaken about the chemistry between me and Edward." I shuffle my feet, "I'd never want him to give up his calling, his profession...for me, you know?"

"And you know the Seven are complicated. If it weren't for the incident, he might never have become a priest."

"What happened to Edward?" I lean forward. "Is that what prompted him to follow this path?"

Summer's forehead creases. "I don't think even the guys know the full story, but what I do know? It's not my story to tell. It's best he tells you himself."

"Of course." My shoulders slump. "So then, what? I wait and watch? That's what you two recommend?"

"Or maybe we could just be friends?" A new voice sounds from behind me. I turn and heat floods my cheek.

"Y-you," I stutter. "What are you doing here?"

# 5

Edward

I stride into the kitchen and the girls glance at each other. The silence stretches and Ava hops from foot to foot. Her face is fiery and she looks like she's about to throw up.

I glance between them and Summer nods. "Uh, Isla and I need to see someone about something."

"What thing?" Isla frowns and Summer nudges her.

Isla blinks rapidly, then straightens, "Oh, yeah, that thing."

Summer begins to haul Isla out of there. Ava watches them leave with a stricken expression. "Uh, I guess I should go too." She turns to follow them.

"Stop, Eve." I hear the authority in my voice and frown. When had I decided it was appropriate to command her to do my bidding? More to the point, why does she respond to my order?

She pauses, but doesn't turn around. Her shoulders are squared, her spine erect.

"Turn around." I force my voice to assume a more normal tone.

This is just a discussion; that's all it is. A conversation. Something I do every day with the people in my parish, so there is nothing different about this. Except there is. None of them resemble this beautiful, innocent creature who was sent my way to tempt me, to show me that I am fallible. To show me that the more I try to resist, the more I will fail. That all this time, while I've taken so much pride in being able to resist any enticement... Apparently, I still have a long way to go. Yeah, that's all this is. A test. Of my morals. My principals. The way of life I have chosen for myself, and I intend to make sure that I pass this. With flying colors.

She slowly turns to face me and the breath rushes out of me.

Without the shield of the blanket that she'd clutched to herself, I see her in the morning light, her Titian hair flowing about her shoulders. Her pale skin gleams in the sunlight that pours over her and haloes her. Her green gaze widens as she takes me in. Color flushes her cheeks, her lips part, and I can't look away. The pink of her lower lip, so soft, it would be so sweet. If I could only taste it once. My foot hits the ground and I realize I've taken a step toward her.

Her gaze widens, she bites down on her lower lip, and the blood rushes to my groin. This can't be happening. And no, no way, am I going to use swear words to give vent to the frustration that wells in my chest. I thrust out my chest, widen my stance. "I heard you, earlier." I fix my gaze on her, and she blushes.

"How...how much of the conversation?" she mumbles.

I tilt my head and her blush deepens.

"Oh, hell." She squeezes her eyes shut. "This is soooo embarrassing." She hunches her shoulders. "I didn't mean to talk about you. I mean, I did, but I was hoping for some clarity, you know? And I can only figure things out if I discuss them."

"You mean, when you are not talking to yourself?"

"Exactly." She snaps her eyes open. "But I swear, you have nothing to worry about."

"No?"

"No." She moves toward me. "Trust me, I have come to a decision."

"Oh?" I lower my chin, "And what would that be?"

She holds out her hand, "Friends."

"Friends?"

"Yeah, you know like the TV series?"

I stare at her and the line between her eyebrows deepens. "You do watch TV, right? I mean, surely, you do know Friends? You know, Rachel and Joey and—"

"I'm a priest, not an ascetic. I haven't renounced the world." *Not completely, that is.*

Her breath hitches, "Sorry. I mean, of course, you know what Friends is. Silly me, why would I think you didn't? Not that I watch it or anything. It's a bit too classic for me. I mean, my older sister loved it and I loved watching it with her, but I tried watching it again recently and it seemed like it hadn't aged well. Unlike you."

"Unlike me?"

She slaps a hand to her forehead, "Did I just say that out loud? How the hell did I let that slip?" She gasps. "Oh, no. I can't believe I just said that." She shakes her head, "Forget it." She swipes her hair over her shoulder. "Can you forget I said that?"

"Not a chance." I draw myself up to my full height. "I take it, you think of me as old?"

She winces. "Not old, but old-*er*."

"How old do you think I am, exactly?"

"Really, I didn't mean anything by that statement."

"How old, Ava?" I infuse enough command in my voice for her to pale. "Tell me."

"Um..." She holds up four fingers, then signals three with her other hand.

"What the—" I explode, "You really think I'm—"

She folds one finger of the first hand, leaving three upright.

"Thirty-three?" I growl, "You think I'm thirty-three?"

"Are you?"

I shake my head, then reach over and fold two fingers of her second hand, leaving only her little finger upright.

Goosebumps pop on her skin, mirroring the ones on mine. I blow out a breath. *Don't swear, don't swear. In fact, don't stay here anymore. Don't look at her. Don't go closer to her again. Turn and leave, if you know what's good for you. And for her. Think about her. Why are you leading her on, when you know there can be no future for either of you together?*

"Thirty-one?" She swallows, "You're thirty-one?"

I nod.

"I'm nineteen." She tucks a strand of hair behind her ear.

I blow out a breath. Of course, I'd sort of guessed that she was young, but I hadn't...couldn't let myself think about it. The proof's right here in front of my eyes though. She's nineteen. *Only nineteen.*

"I know you think that I'm too young, but you are wrong," she declares.

"I am?"

She nods. "I was born an old soul, and I promise you, I am tougher than I look. I'm more persistent than people give me credit for."

"Is that right?"

"Don't you believe me?" She draws herself up to her full height, which still means she barely reaches my chest. So young, so delicate, so tiny. A gift from the heavens to coax me along the right path. *Which is what?* Return to my duties, stay true to my chosen route. Don't let anything distract me from my obligations, my responsibilities to my flock. Yes, that's why she's come into my life. To show me how unsuited I am to a world where temptations lurk around every corner... I'd never be able to resist them. I'd lose myself in them again, I'd lose my clarity of thinking, my soul...and that, I cannot bear. Not again.

"It's not you I doubt; it's me."

She blinks.

"It's not your words I'm unsure of; it's my thoughts."

She swallows.

I take a step forward and the scent of jasmine clouds my senses. The band around my chest tightens. I raise my hand toward her and her breathing grows harsher.

"It's not your persistence that I question; it's my ability to stay true to myself that I have reservations about."

I make the sign of the cross, then walk past her. I head for the exit, when she calls out, "Edward."

The sound of my name from her lips sends my pulse racing. I fist my fingers at my sides, then pause.

Footsteps thud, she draws abreast, then plants herself in my path.

"You believe in a higher power, don't you? So, do I. I believe there's a reason we are drawn to each other. And while I can't claim to understand why, I am willing to be patient to find out. Meanwhile, I really do want us to be friends." She holds out her hand, "Please, Edward."

I glance down at her hand, then at her face.

"We can never be friends."

Brushing past her, I walk out.

# 6

Ava

I stare at my reflection in the mirror of the dressing room allocated to me. My first gig. My FIRST gig. Whoa. It's for a destination wedding Isla is organizing. The entire theme is a mix of exotica drawing on different influences from the East. They'd wanted a performance to kick off the evening's festivities, which is where I come in. Isla had asked me and I'd jumped at the opportunity. Finally, I am moving forward in the direction of my dreams.

I take in the beaded appliqué work of my blouse, the tiny mirrors sewn into it reflecting the light from the bulbs that frame the mirror. My hips are encased in a pair of shorts, attached to long panels of light, gossamer fabric that falls to my ankles. Intricate overlays of sequins catch the light and shimmer. I stare at my reflection and can't stop the smile that traces my lips.

I'd only been twelve when I'd attended a musical and watched the women shaking their hips. With the colored scarfs that they'd wrapped around their hips, their hair open and rippling down their backs, their laughter and happy faces as they'd flung their heads back, shaken their arms and legs, and moved to a rhythm I'd sensed but not heard—I'd felt a primitive calling to be one of them. To be as free, to not think, to be able to live in the moment as I allow the music to take over, to let my body flow with the beats.

My mother had loved everything to do with the East. Even though she had been dead set against my career as a dancer, it was she who'd influenced my eclectic taste in music. I reach for my purse on the dressing table, pull out the picture I keep in its protective sleeve. It's of the four of us—Mum, Dad, me and Raisa. I touch my finger to Mum's smiling face. She looked so young, so happy there. I love this picture, taken on one of the many summer vacations we'd spent exploring the countryside, wearing my favorite red dress, a gift from Mum. It's the only picture I took with me when I left home. I had been angry and grieving at Mum's death, the loss too much to bear.

Had even wondered if the disappointment in my career choice had brought on the cancer. But my sister had banished the notion. It was Raisa who had encouraged me to follow my dream when my parents had been so against my dropping out of med school. She'd told me that if my heart lay in dancing, then I should follow it. If I didn't try, I'd never know what was right for me.

I'd taken her advice, and never regretted it. If only I could bring some of that courage to bear on the upcoming solo performance. My first solo performance. Gah!

There's a knock on the door and Isla pops her head into the room, "Five minutes, babe."

I nod as she closes the door behind her, then slide the picture back inside my handbag. This is it. I can do this. I have to do this. If I have any hope of competing in the World Belly Dancing Championships that will be held in a few months, then I have to start with conquering my fear of live performances, which begins with this one. Of course, I do have to actually sign up for the competition, which I will do... Just as soon as I get my courage together.

I rise to my feet, walk out toward the stage that's been erected in one corner of the ballroom of the Dorchester Hotel. It's the most exclusive hotel in town, also owned by Saint, one of the Seven.

The sound of guests talking and cutlery clinking against plates reaches me as I step on the stage. I walk to the center of the platform, take my stance. Wait... Wait...as the noise ebbs...flows...begins to die down. A hush creeps through the audience and I still don't move. I keep my sight focused on a distant point at the back of the room. Silence descends, yet I still wait. A beat, then another. The first strains of the music I'd chosen for this piece drift through the air. *Where Have You Been* by Rihanna.

The notes swirl around me, sink into my blood as I sway my hips, twitch the muscles of my stomach, raise my arms in the air, and allow the notes to guide me. I close my eyes, let myself sink into the rhythm, swirl my hips, move my feet, glide my arms down to my hips, lower still, curve my spine and raise my arms above me, then straighten to twirl around and around. I dance to the beats until I am sweating and limber.

My joints loose, my skin warm from the exertion, sweat beads my forehead and trickles down my back. Finally, I leap through the air, land on my feet, roll, and sink to one knee, head bowed.

The music fades away.

In the silence that follows, my heart beat drums in my ears, blood pumps at my wrists, behind my eyes. My heart thunders in my chest —*clap-clap-clap*—the sound of the audience's applause echoes the rhythm.

"*Bravo.*"

"*Encore.*"

I allow my lips to curve in a huge smile. I did it. Yes. I pulled it off. Maybe, just maybe, I'll be able to make a career out of this, after all.

The hair on the back of my neck rises. My pulse rate ratchets up. I tip my head up, glance about at the smiling faces of the audience until my gaze clashes with his.

Amber eyes, burning brightly, fringed with those incredibly dark, thick lashes that I want to feel feather across my skin.

I swallow; my throat dries. A bead of sweat trails down my spine as I hold his gaze and I struggle to maintain my composure, despite the tickle. His lips firm and a nerve throbs at his temple. He narrows his gaze and the skin around his lips tightens. No doubt about it, he's angry. But why? What the hell did I do to warrant his ire? What do I even care if I did? I tip up my chin, then rise to my feet. I rake my gaze down that perfect nose, across his gorgeously shaped lips, the tendons of his throat that are constricted by the white collar he wears at his neck.

*Oh.* My stomach hollows out and my palms dampen. Of course, he's here in an official capacity. Likely, he officiated the wedding ceremony that took place earlier.

I raise my gaze to his, and the coldness in his eyes seems to deepen. He wipes all expression from his face, draws himself up to his full height, which puts him heads and shoulders above everyone else in the vicinity.

His shoulders bunch, the fabric of his long-sleeved black shirt stretches across his massive chest. His biceps bulge and strain the seams. He seems to be in the throes of some emotion that I can't quite identify.

I tilt my chin up, thrust out my hip and place my palm on it.

His jaw tightens. Then he turns on his heel and marches off.

*What the hell —?*

The crowd swallows him, people clapping and whistling. The sound washes over me. There's a touch on my shoulder and I shudder. I glance up into Isla's concerned gaze. "You, okay? You look like you've seen a ghost."

Or the devil... Which can't be right, because he's the exact opposite. Right? A man who's devoted himself to the service of God. So why the hell can't I get past this attraction I feel toward him? And it's not only because his name is Edward. This is something deeper, more powerful. More forbidden. Is it because I am not supposed to entertain such images about him that I can't stop myself from thinking along those lines?

*Oh, my god!* I snort. And God can't do anything for me right now, because he's the one who put me in this position.

"I'm okay." Or I will be, as soon as I wash off the sweat from this bout of dancing. And shed the impure thoughts that crowd my mind, and which I have no right to be thinking. To think, I can't even confess them aloud...because hell, there's no one else I'd rather be confessing to than the glowering, growling, grumpy man who'd clearly watched me dance and not been too happy about it. Well, too bad. Bugger him and his judgmental ass. I can do what I want, when I want, as long as it makes me happy. And right now, dancing is the only thing that seems to give me some sense of myself. Which is what I want, right?

A few of the men and women from the crowd step onto the platform and I clutch at Isla's arm. "I know it's not being very polite, considering this is a private gig and I do need more of these, but right now, would you mind very much if I went back to my room? I just need a break."

"From him, you mean?" She jerks her chin in the direction of where the glowering jerkass—argh, is it wrong to think of a priest in those terms? —had stood.

"You saw him?" I whisper.

"Hard to miss, when he glared at you all through your performance." Isla chuckles.

"Shit." I hunch my shoulders. Good thing I hadn't noticed him until the very end of the performance or there's no telling what would have happened. I'd have lost my rhythm, most likely, and that...is saying a lot. Once I start a dance routine, normally, nothing can distract me...but I suspect he could. The crowd of people reach us. I turn around, head the other way, leaving Isla to manage them.

That woman is a keeper, seriously. The way she'd pulled off the reception for Arpad and Karina in a very short period of time—I'm talking days, here—was a miracle. She never loses her cool, always manages to get things organized. If only I could get her to organize my life, as well. I veer down the corridor and back to the hotel room that doubles as my dressing room.

Slipping inside, I place the bouquet on the dresser. Then shake back the hair from my face. Turning, I head for the bathroom, step inside to run the shower. I slide down one side of my blouse when the hair on my nape stands to attention again. I glance up and meet his gaze in the mirror.

Somehow, I am not surprised. After the way Isla had said he'd watched me through that performance, it was inevitable that he would follow me here.

I stare as he watches me from the doorway of the bath. Shit, is he going to come in? Why isn't he coming in?

I raise my shoulder and allow the sleeve of my blouse to slip further down my arm.

His chest rises and falls. He watches me with a searing intensity that sends a frisson of lust chasing down my spine, straight to that part of me between my thighs. My core clenches. Moisture pools between my legs, dots my palms. And it's not because of the steam from the shower.

I reach behind me to undo the ties of my blouse when he puts up a hand. "Stop," he commands and all of my pores seem to pop.

I halt with my hand on the knot that holds the edges of my bodice together, watch him as he curls his fingers at his sides, as his chest muscles ripple, and he drags his fingers through his hair, before whipping off his priest's collar and shoving it in his pocket.

Umm, okay, not what I expected.

He walks over to stand right behind me. The heat from his body sears me. The steam from the shower in front creates a fine mist that seems to dot his forehead, cling to the crisp collar of his shirt, now open to reveal the tendons of his beautiful throat. My belly flutters and my toes curl. What craziness is this that just the sight of his throat seems to send me into raptures of the kind I've never faced before? My fingers itch and my palms ache. I want to step back, close the distance between us and rub the curves of my ass against that thick, heavy length of his that would be tenting his pants about now. And I shouldn't do that. I blow out a breath, then move toward the sink. I hook my fingers over the edge of the sink, tip my chin up to hold his gaze in the mirror.

"Why are you here, Edward?"

# 7

Edward

That's the question I'm asking myself. I shouldn't be here. What the hell am I doing here? I'd walked away from her the last time, determined to stay away from her. Then I'd stayed on after officiating the wedding, and seen her dance.

She'd moved her hips, her waist, bowed her body so gracefully to the music, allowed the notes to take over, had drawn the rhythm into her body and embodied the essence of the music. Hot, passionate, yet deep and soul-stirring. That's her. When she dances, she transcends the physical. She embodies the melody, becomes one with the tune... the chords...the notes... To see her dance is as much of a spiritual experience as when I pray to Him above. I clench my fists at my sides.

How can I do this? How can I compare what I have with my Savior to how I felt when I watched her? Why did I have to follow her from the performance and into her hotel room?

"How did you get in?" she whispers.

"The door," I jerk my chin toward the entrance to the room. "It hadn't closed completely."

And I had walked in and invaded her privacy. Why had I thought I could simply barge in here unannounced? More to the point, what had I been thinking anyway? Why had I thought it was okay to push the door open and step in? What's wrong with me? Why is it that when I see her, I seem to lose my head completely?

I squeeze my eyes closed, turn to leave, when she grabs my hand. Sensations vibrate out from the point of contact. I glance down at where her fingers are curled around my wrist.

I glance up at her and she releases me. "Sorry," she mutters, "I... I don't want you to leave."

And I don't want to go, and that is the problem. But I don't say that aloud.

Instead, I stare past her at the open door of the shower cubicle, "Why don't you finish your shower? I'll wait out here."

"You sure?" she asks.

I frown at her and she reddens.

"I didn't mean it that way. I mean, I do want you to wait. It's not that I wanted you to join me or anything. I mean—" She slaps her hand to her forehead. "Oh, hell, forget what I said. I mean—"

"I know what you mean." I can't stop the smile that quirks my lips. "Why don't you go on?" I jerk my chin toward the shower. "I'll be right outside."

I pivot, then step out and pull the door closed behind me.

I walk over to the window, pull back the curtains, and glance down at the road below. Just two streets up, the tourists and shoppers crowd Oxford Circus. You'd think there would be lots of traffic near the most exclusive hotel in London, but surprisingly, down here there are no vehicles, and almost no pedestrian traffic. Except for what seems to be a homeless man who sits on the sidewalk, almost right below the window. He seems to be holding up a sign as well...the letters of which are hidden from my line of sight. Hmm, given this is one of the most exclusive hotels in the city, it's strange the hotel allows him to stay there. Not to mention, it can't be a lucrative spot for him without foot traffic.

The sound of the shower running reaches me. I turn toward it, and of course, my imagination goes straight to her under the water, without clothes, the droplets running down her breasts, her stomach, to the place between her thighs. I shake my head, grab the rosary out of my pocket, sink to my knees and cross myself. Then I begin to pray.

*I believe in God, the Father Almighty, Creator of Heaven and earth and in Jesus Christ, His only Son, our Lord...*

I repeat the prayer, until all thoughts exit my head and my mind stills. My heart beat slows down, my muscles relax, and my breathing stabilizes.

I stay there until I hear the sound of her footsteps. Then I open my eyes, and rise to my feet.

She walks toward me, wearing a white dress, her auburn hair freshly washed and flowing down her back. Light pours out of the bathroom, turning the fabric translucent, creating a halo around her. I take in the curves of her body. The highlights in her hair that glisten and sparkle as she moves.

She resembles an otherworldly vision, an angel who's arrived on earth to tease me, to test me...to reveal the error of my ways. She pauses in front of me, tips her chin up.

"Hello," she says softly, "hope I didn't keep you waiting."

*You can keep me waiting forever, for that's the way it's going to be between us. I can't touch you, can't hold you, can't allow myself to think of you, but what I can give you is "friendship."* I roll the word around my tongue, "You wanted us to be friends. I accept that."

"You do?" She frowns. "I thought you said we could never be friends."

"What I meant was that we could never be *just* friends."

She scowls, folds her arms about her waist. "Then what—?"

I raise my hand and she purses her lips.

"I thought it would be best if we didn't see each other at all. If I didn't allow myself anywhere near you, there wouldn't be any temptation. But I was wrong."

"You were?"

I nod, "I realize now, you were sent to me precisely so I could continuously test myself. You are the route to my betterment. Before you, I'd become boring... Complacent, even. I'd reached a plateau, where I thought I was doing everything I could to show the Lord that I am his faithful disciple, but it turns out that I was wrong."

She glowers at me. "You were, huh?"

"Yes. Absolutely." I square my shoulders. "You are His way of showing me that I have a long way to go before I master my senses. I thought I'd conquered my weaknesses, but now I can see that's not true."

"So," she straightens, "I am a weakness?"

"Exactly." I nod. "You're a failing, someone sent to hold a mirror up to my shortcomings."

"Shortcomings?" She huffs, "You're calling me a shortcoming?"

"Not you." I frown. "Mine, I am the one found wanting. I saw you and realized just how long a road I have yet to travel before I can claim to be anywhere near the kind of perfection I hope to achieve."

"You are trying to achieve perfection, huh?"

"Aren't we all?" I drawl.

"Not me, buster." She shakes her hair back from her face. "I am human, and I plan to embrace my failings, my imperfections and my quirks, without which I am nothing but a colorless shadow of myself."

"You," I chuckle, "you'll never be a colorless anything. You're fire and radiance and purity—the kind I can only hope to achieve."

She opens and shuts her mouth. "Purity?" She shakes her head. "You're confusing me with someone else."

"I know what I see..." I rake my gaze across her features, "a woman who's passionate about what she believes, who wants to live life to the fullest, who wants to experience every single experience, every emotion there is. Someone who—"

She reaches forward and slaps her palm over my mouth. "Stop," she whispers.

Sensations curl in my chest and blood rushes to my groin. I step back.

She pulls back her hand. "Sorry." She hesitates. "I... I didn't mean to do that, but sometimes when I'm with you, it's difficult for me to hold back."

"That's what I mean." I spear my fingers through my hair. "Clearly, this is why we need to meet. It's the only way I can continuously test myself against the temptation that you embody. You're an impulse I need to steer clear of. An enticement I must...avoid at all costs."

She blinks rapidly. "Okay, now I am completely confused. You want to avoid me... Yet you say we need to meet. But earlier, you said we shouldn't be friends. So, what is it?"

"I'm saying, we should be friends with benefits."

She gapes. "Benefits?" she chokes out. "What...what kind of benefits?"

"The conversational kind."

"Excuse me?"

"You heard me." I quirk my lips. "We meet, keep our distance," I point to the space between us, "but we continue to converse, to exchange opinions on anything under the sun."

"And during the time we meet, you try to resist me?"

"Exactly." I snap my fingers. "What better way to prove myself to the Lord than to show that I can withstand the wickedest of lures that he sends my way?"

"That's it." She throws up her hands, "First, you raise me up on some kind of bullshit pedestal that I definitely don't deserve. Then, you compare me to being some kind of sin. You know what? Forget it!"

She turns, heads toward the table in the corner and begins to stuff her clothes into her bag.

My heart begins to hammer; my pulse pounds at my temples. Hold on, what did I do wrong? I simply shared with her what I was thinking. Had I been wrong in that? Isn't it best to be upfront in these situations? What had I said that could evoke such a reaction from her anyway?

"Ava," I head toward her, "You're not acting in a sane manner. All I'm saying is, let's be friends and talk openly when we meet."

"To hell with that." She huffs, "I don't want anything to do with that, Father. You're a...a...completely self-absorbed prick, as far as I am concerned. How can you be a priest and serve your people if you can't even understand how it is to be in my shoes and be attracted to you...you...?" she heaves her bag over her shoulder and turns on me, "you who are already committed to someone else, and I can't stop thinking of you? Do you realize how horrible that makes me feel? And then you have the nerve to tell me that I am your test? Your trial, your bloody experiment... And all so what? You can prove to yourself that you are perfect? Well, sod that," she turns and heads for the door, "and sod you, Father."

*Stop her, go to her, explain to her how difficult this is for you as well.* Explain that you realized if you couldn't have any other relationship with her, being a friend could, at least, mean that you'd have her in your life. That you'd have a chance to, at least, see her, talk to her, hear her laugh again. Even though every moment in her presence brings home the fact that you can't have her. Can't be with her. Can't have anything to do with her. And all those explanations earlier... Well, they are just rationalizations for my actions.

She wrenches open the door and I call out to her, "Ava, stop. Please don't leave like this."

"I don't want to stay on when I'm clearly not needed. Why did you come here, Edward? Why couldn't you have left earlier?"

"Because I couldn't." I shuffle my feet, "I had to...see you once more."

"But why?" She firms her lips. "Tell me, why it was so important that you meet me?"

"Because..." I take a step froward, stop, then fold my fingers into fists at my sides, "because I will not act on my impulses, Ava. I will not allow you or anyone or anything else to come in the way of my chosen path, and if that means I have to use you to make a point to myself, then so be it."

Color drains from her face, then she grips the strap over her shoulder even tighter. "Well, you know what? I am not a...a test...or a trial or an experiment... I am a living, breathing woman, and there are many out there who'll take me for what I am, and cherish me and love me."

She hunches her shoulders, and the movement dislodges her scarf which floats to the floor.

"And I may have thought that perhaps there was a connection between us... And maybe I thought you might do something about it, that you'd, at least, be honest with yourself that it means something," she swallows, "something more than turning it into...this... Tool to prove to yourself just how strong you are and how perfect you can be."

A cold sensation stabs at my chest and my guts twist. What have I done? Why couldn't I have listened better to her? Why couldn't I have understood my own emotions more clearly? Why couldn't I have been more receptive to what she had to say? Why did I have to go and mis-interpret everything? Have I, though? Am I really that off-target? Am I really incorrect in seeing this situation for what it is? A chance to find out how committed I am to my chosen path?

I widen my stance, thrust out my chest, "I'm sorry you see it that way."

"Me too."

She turns to leave, when I call out again, "Ava." I walk toward her scarf, pick it up and hold it out. "I think this belongs to you."

"Keep it. Perhaps it'll be a reminder of what you refused to recognize between us." Turning, she walks out.

# 8

Ava

"He said what...?" Isla opens and closes her mouth. Clearly, she's as shocked as me. Unlike her, I've had a few days to process what Edward had tried to convey to me. The gist of it was... Nothing comes close to the relationship he's already consecrated with the One Above. I am a distraction. What had he called me? An irritant, someone who got in his way, someone he'd use as a means to test out how strong his resistance to temptation is.

"I mean, should I, perhaps, be flattered that he sees me as some kind of trial by fire?" I chew on my lower lip. "Maybe I should give him credit for trying to do what's right?"

"Right for you or for him?" She huffs up the slope of Waterlow Park. We're in my favorite green space is in the heart of London...not far from the house I am renting. It's a one-bedroom, tiny place, rundown enough that I could snag a short term let on my shoestring budget.

"Right for both of us?" I hunch into my jacket. A gust of wind blows the hair into my face and I push it away. "I mean, I do under-stand where he's coming from... Kind of..."

"Do you...?" She turns to me, "You're a better woman than I, Sherlock."

"Umm...isn't that dialogue supposed to refer to Shylock?"

She waves a hand in the air, "Same thing."

"It's not." I laugh.

"Just as it's not cool that he actually mentioned to you that he wanted to be friends with you only so he could use you as a test."

"At least, he was open about it." I rub my hands together, then blow on them. Shit, it's February but the weather shows no sign of improvement. "I mean, if he'd acted on impulse and tried to kiss me or something... Now that...wouldn't have been cool, considering who he is."

"Do you want him to kiss you?"

"What do you think?" I reach the pinnacle of the slope, then turn to take in the sight of all of London stretched out in front of me. Which means it is largely flat... Except for the tall buildings in the distance, which constitute the city.

"I think," Isla pants as she lurches up to the flat stretch of space at the top, then pivots to stand next to me, "that you want to do more than that, regardless of the fact that he's a priest. Not that I blame you; he's freakin' hot." She fans her hand in front of her face. "And right now, the only one of the Seven who's not attached."

"What about Baron?" I frown, "Isn't he also unmarried?"

"Who knows with Baron?" She bounces on the balls of her feet in a bid to warm herself. "From what the rest tell me, they have no idea what he's up to. They only know he's alive because he sent a letter of congratulations to Arpad and Karina at their wedding."

"So, they do know where he is?"

"Nope." She shakes her head. "He only uses snail mail. There's a PO Box where they can reach him, but other than that, they have no idea what he's been up to all these years."

"So, he doesn't want to keep in touch with the others?"

"Well, I'm told he's still one of the co-owners of 7A investments, the company that the Seven own together... So presumably, he's able to access the money that they make for him to live on."

"You know a lot about the Seven, huh?"

"Only because they've been keeping me busy, planning their weddings. Those alphaholes," she shakes her head, "they spend their days fighting their attraction to their women, only to fall harder and then, can't wait to get married, very often overnight." She wraps her hair around her palms and tugs. "Honestly, the kind of stress they've put me through to find the right venues and book them, not to mention arrange everything else at the drop of a hat, it's a wonder I haven't had a cardiac."

She thumps her palm against her chest.

"Good thing there's only Edward left," Isla mutters, "and clearly, he's not getting married."

"There's Baron," I remind her. "Also, how can you be sure?"

"Baron's missing, so I'm not counting him." She scowls at me, "And Edward's a priest, and considering what he just told you, you can safely cross him off the list of potential boyfriends."

"Can I?" I turn away, stare at the now partially-clouded-by-fog view of London in the distance. "I mean, just because he's a priest... And rude, not to mention, obnoxious..."

"There's also a small matter of," she points a finger in the direction of the skies, "you know, the relationship he has with the One Above."

"Tell me about it." I dig the heels of my boot into the ground. "I am sure I'm committing some kind of sin just by thinking of him in the way I am, but darn it, I can't get him out of my mind."

"Not even after how he treated you the other day?"

"Especially after how he treated me the other day." I shoot her a sideways glance. "Does that make me...stupid? Or just someone who loves punishment... Or maybe I simply have irrational expectations from this entire situation."

She closes the distance between us, grips my shoulder. "I know all about what it feels like to be attracted to the wrong man."

"Umm," I scowl at her, "something you wanna tell me?'

She blows out a breath, "Nope, just saying, that I empathize."

"Hmm, well, not much I can do about it, considering what's-his-face has told me there's no future for us. Not that I expected there to be. I mean, he's a priest." My shoulders slump. "Shit, this is sooo wrong on so many levels."

"Easy, babe." She pats my shoulder. "No harm done. It's not like the two of you acted on the itch or anything. You only thought about it, which hell... Nothing anyone can do about it. I mean, it's not like he can peek into your head and punish you for your thoughts, right?"

"Umm," I scowl, "isn't the whole point that God can, in fact, peek into your head and punish you for your thoughts?"

"I guess," she shrugs, "but you know what I mean?"

"No," I shake my head, "explain it to me."

"Well, I mean... So maybe the One Above knows your thoughts, but he's not telling anyone, is he?"

"No, I'm doing a damn good job of that myself." I gesture between us.

"What you need is a distraction from all this. Maybe a night on the town, let your hair down."

"I think I'd prefer to go back to my studio, practice another routine that I'll be teaching soon." I swipe my hair over my shoulder, "I really need to focus on my career at this stage, you know?"

"Is that what you want?" She tilts her head.

"Don't you?"

"I want a successful career, for sure, and I want to make it on my own, but every success I've had only makes it seem even more hollow, makes me want to reach for the next one. I don't think I've ever taken the time to appreciate what I have, you know? And sometimes it makes me wonder if it's all worth it."

"Wow," I blink, "and I thought I was the boring introspective one here."

"That you are." She smirks. "Boring and introspective and way too beautiful for your own good."

"Aww, come on." I poke a finger into her shoulder. "Who are you and what have you done to my fun-loving friend?"

"Fun-loving, sex starved friend, who's not had any action in..." She counts on her fingers, "Whoa, has it been that long?" She pales. "No wonder my vagina is dictating my thoughts."

"Thought that only applied to men." I chuckle. "Besides, I can't weigh in on it. I've never—" Color floods my cheeks. "Shit, forget I said anything. Do you want a drink? I want a drink; shall we go to the pub—"

"Holdonabloodysecond." Isla stares at me, "Are you saying?" She shakes her head. "Nope, it can't be. Tell me it's not true. I mean, I know you're only nineteen, still...you know...I thought..."

"Shut up." I blush harder. "Seriously, Iz, lay off. It's not something I want to talk about."

"Are you holding out for the 'one'?" She punctuates the last word with air-quotes. "Is that why you haven't slept with anyone so far?"

"Not like don't have any experience... I do know how to use my vibrator properly, thank you very much." I laugh.

Isla rolls her eyes. "Not the same as being with a man..." She rakes her gaze over my features, "It's also the intimacy, you know. That's what I miss the most. Not that the men in my life have excelled at that in any way either... Still, it was better than nothing," she purses her lips, "I suppose."

"You don't sound very convinced."

"All I can say is that I haven't yet been with someone who can rock my world, the way I read about it in romance novels—"

"Those kind of alpha males don't exist," I mutter. "Romance novels were dreamed up by women who, clearly, know how to spin a fantasy. It's why I never read them."

"What?" she screeches. "You haven't read any romance novels?"

I stare at her, and she chuckles, "Good one."

"Not." I pout. "I am addicted to them," I mutter. "How someone who started out with Twilight graduated to the kind of smut I read now, I'll never know. I singularly blame them for my addiction to a certain man who's completely unsuited to my needs."

"Now I see why he's so attracted to you."

"You do?"

She nods, "It's the combination of the little virgin façade, combined with the curves of Venus, which hides the heart of a little slut."

"Whoa," I blink, "I'm not sure who you are talking about here?"

"You, babe." She laughs. "You. Bet he looks at you and sees a little sacrificial lamb that he can't wait to sink his teeth into."

I stiffen. "You make me sound like some kind of...of..."

"Sinful dish?" she offers.

"I thought you were suggesting he was a vampire." I pout. "And now you're agreeing with him. Seriously, this is all kinds of screwed up. I need to take my mind off Edward completely." I straighten. "Yeah, that's what I should do. I need to find someone to sleep with. That will take my mind off Edward completely."

She frowns, "Don't do anything rash. Maybe you should think things through first. Sleep on it some more—"

"I'd rather sleep with someone else. I bet that will put things in perspective."

I pivot, brush past the others crowded at the peak of the hill.

"Where are you going?" she calls out as she rushes to catch up with me.

"To the bar, to get a drink and see if I can't find someone to shag tonight." I hurry down the slope, then turn to find her standing in place, her mouth hanging open. I wave my arm and beckon to her, "Aren't you coming with me?"

# 9

Edward

I step into the chancel of the church via the priest's door. The long sleeves of my cassock fit around my arms; my collar is snug around my neck, a reminder of the One to whom I belong. The One who'd saved me when I'd most needed Him. When I'd been doped out of my head on drugs, and a part of me had wondered what it would be like to end it all. When I'd floated in that strange out of body space, and turned toward the light in the distance; the realization had sunk in then. I wasn't alone. All I had to do was surrender to the fate that had brought me that far. However much I'd abused my system with drugs, I couldn't kill myself. Perhaps there was a reason to everything that had happened... Perhaps there was something more ahead, something I couldn't see yet. A future that was not what I had imagined, but a future nevertheless. One in which I could be of service to others.

That's when I'd surrendered to my His plan, and for the first time in my life, I'd prayed. I'd asked Him to show me the way, to tell me what to do next. How could I crawl out of the web of misery that bound my every move, that trapped me? And the answer had seeped into my soul. Live. Not for you, but for them. The people you can help, the world you can change, the children who need your love and your guidance, the souls you can help guide. Live for them.

And I had.

I sink down to my knees in front of the altar, press my palms together, bow my head. *Blessed Lord above, forgive me for I have sinned. Forgive me for I forsook You when I was tempted. Forgive me for straying from the path. Forgive me for doubting myself, and hence, doubting You. Forgive me for the sins I have committed, and for those I am yet to commit. Forgive me, for I blinked and looked away. Forgive me, for I was distracted by her beauty. Her grace. For I allowed myself to be swayed by the thoughts of flesh, by the thoughts of how it would be to not be alone. For I am not, not really, not when You are with me for every breath I take. Forgive me for being disloyal to You. Forgive me for contemplating a life without You. For there is none. This is all there is. Me at Your service to do Your bidding, to follow Your directives. Bid me, Lord, for I am Your humble servant. I surrender to You and I will accept any punishment that You bestow.* I swallow down the emotions that block my throat. *Speak to me, Lord. Tell me You forgive me; tell me You have not deserted me for my actions. Tell me You pardon the sins I committed by thinking of someone else other than You. Please my Lord, talk to me. Are You still angry with me? Do You not forgive me? I—*

"I forgive you."

The voice slides through the thoughts in my head. I jerk my head up, open my eyes, stare up at the marble figure high above. The stillness, the tranquility, the beauty of His pathos sink into my soul. My heart begins to race; my pulse pounds. I gaze up and into the face of the one who has held my thoughts for so many years now.

"Even though you don't deserve it." The voice sounds from behind me. I pivot and watch as Sterling approaches.

I draw in a breath and his lips quirk. "You didn't think it was the Man above speaking to you now, did you?"

I squeeze my eyes shut. *Yes, I had.* And for a few seconds there, I had been convinced that He had answered. Even though, deep inside, I've always known that I must love Him without expectation, simply knowing that He loves, despite everything.

I turn back to the altar, make the sign of the cross, then rise up to my feet. "Sinclair, what brings the Sinner himself into the house of Christ?"

"You, Father."

"Me?" I turn to him. "Now, that's something I'd never thought I'd hear from you. Is there something I can help you with?"

"The question is, can you help me help you, Father?"

I tilt my head. "And I thought I was the preacher here."

"There's a spark of the divine in all of us, Father."

I chuckle. "You're a canny one. How did Summer manage to hold you down long enough to put a ring on your finger?" I jerk my chin to where the platinum band encircles his left ring finger.

He places the finger so his right hand is over his left, plays with the ring. "This? If you recall, I didn't have one in time for our wedding, but Summer wanted me to wear it and if it makes her happy… Well," he raises his shoulders, "but I am not here to talk about me."

"Too bad," I widen my stance, "when I was sure you were finally here to repent for your sins."

He chuckles, "That would take more time than we have today."

"Oh?" I frown. "I wasn't aware we were on a timetable."

"The only one that counts, Father." He gestures toward the door that leads out into the garden, "Shall we?"

I frown. "I'm not done here yet."

"You'll have enough time to commune with God, once we've had our conversation."

"That sounds...ominous. Should I be worried?" I glower.

"I don't know, Father. Should you?" He holds my gaze.

I don't back down.

Neither does he.

Finally, he steps back, "Look, ten minutes of your time. That's all I ask."

"Hmm," I rub the back of my neck, "not that I don't trust you—"

"My ego would be bruised if you did." He chuckles.

"But you are here, and I never turn away anyone who asks me for help."

"Is that what you think?" His lips kick up.

"Isn't that what this is?"

"Technically, I need you to help me help you, so," he shrugs, "I suppose that would work." He jerks his chin toward the garden, "Come on, Father, let's talk."

I step forward and he follows me through the priest's door and into the room behind. I step into my office, then come to a stop. Sprawled around the space are four other figures. I groan. "Is this what I think it is?"

"What do you think it is?" Saint drawls from his perch on my desk.

Behind me, Sinclair shuts the door and locks it. I glance at him over my shoulder to see him fold his arms over his chest. Guess leaving that way is out—not that I am going to try it. I'm not a coward. This is only about facing my friends and talking to them, something I'm good at. After all, I've done it so many times before, right?

"I think, if you guys wanted to talk to me, you could have called."

"We did." Damian, picks up my phone, from where I'd left it charging on a side table in the far corner. "What's the use of having a phone, if you don't carry it?"

"I had other things on my mind."

"I'll bet." Arpad pushes away from his corner. He walks over to stand in front of me, "It's what we're here to talk to you about."

"That's my dialogue, surely." I laugh. "Every time one of you guys had a crisis, guess who was there to talk some sense into you?"

The others stare at me.

"Exactly." I nod.

"Exactly." Arpad smirks.

"Exactly." Damian chuckles.

I pause, glance around at their faces. "No." I stiffen. "No, no, no, I think it's time you guys left."

"I think it's time we find out what's happening with you." Saint smirks.

"Me?" I hold out my arms, "I'm just fine."

"You don't look fine." Weston scratches his jaw. "You look like you need to get something off your chest."

"What do you think I was doing just then?" I stab my thumb over my shoulder.

"Praying?" Sinclair frowns. He prowls over to stare at the cross high up on the wall. "Not that we can compete with the man up there. But hey, if He is your Father, we are your brothers...almost...so—"

"Hold on a second." I stare. "Is this you, Sinclair Sterling, pulling the bro-card on me?"

"Is it working?" He smirks at me over his shoulder.

"Not sure." I fold my arms over my chest, "When you guys hunt in a pack like this, it can be quite overwhelming."

"Welcome to the other side, bro." Arpad laughs. "You did us all a favor... Well, all except Baron, considering he missed all the good stuff."

I stiffen. "Let's not talk about Baron, shall we?"

"Agreed," Saint drawls. "Why don't we talk, instead, about what's been causing you to go infinite laps in the pool."

"Who told you that?" I frown. There's no change of expression on Sinclair's face, but his eyes gleam.

I blow out a breath. "Summer told you?"

He tilts his head.

"What did she say?" I demand. "It was simply one interaction by the pool—"

"When all you had on was your Speedo—"

"You went swimming in February in an outdoor pool?" Weston stares.

"When do you swim? In December?" I snap.

Weston shakes his head. "Ask a stupid question, get a stupid answer—"

"Don't change the topic, Ed." Sinclair prowls over to me. "You also had a conversation with her in the kitchen of my place."

"Where the girls were listening in..." I raise my eyes skyward. "Of course, they were."

"Before that, she met you at the guesthouse."

"Hey," I scowl, "you keeping tabs on me, or what?"

"And don't forget the wedding encounter." Damian smirks.

"It's Isla." I straighten. "She's the one who's been sneaking information to you."

"So, there is something to sneak, then?" Saint prowls over to me, "It's confession time, Ed. Tell us what's on your mind."

I glare around the room, take in the faces of my friends, the closest I have to family, my brothers, the ones who have had my back since the incident. "Yes." I rotate my shoulders. "Actually, there is something I need to tell you guys."

Saint straightens and steps away from the desk. Damian places my phone back on the table and gives me his full attention. Sinclair, Weston and Arpad glance at me, their expressions ranging from curious to intrigued.

"This is it then?" Saint finally says, "You're ready to tell us about what's crawled up your craw?"

"I am." I widen my stance. "Baron; he's coming back."

# 10

Edward

Silence descends on the room, then Arpad bursts out, "Did I just hear you say—?"

"Baron?" Damian scowls.

"He's returning?" Weston drums his fingers on his chest.

I nod.

"When?" Saint snaps.

"He didn't give specifics. All he said was that we need to be extra vigilant because we are closing in on the perpetrators behind our kidnapping."

"Ah," Arpad snaps his fingers, "so the information Antonio's been sending us is correct then?"

Arpad's referring to one of the Sicilian Mafia who is also one of our informants.

"How the hell does Baron keep track of everything that's happening from wherever he is?" Saint mutters. "You'd think he has someone keeping an eye on us."

Silence in the room. The men look at each other, then Sinclair widens his stance. "Wouldn't put it past the bastard." He scowls.

"Not that it matters." Damian shrugs. "We don't have anything to hide from him. If he kept in touch with us, we'd simply share everything anyway."

"How did Baron contact you, Ed?" Sinclair finally asks. "The last time we heard from him was when—"

"—he wrote me with advice for Damian, telling him not to marry Julia," Arpad takes up from where Sinclair left off.

"Knowing full well that's exactly what I would do as a result," Damian mutters.

"And now he's written to you, saying he's coming back?" Sinclair frowns.

"Because what, he knows Edward is in a similar quandary of the heart?" Damian asks.

"I am not in any quandary." I draw in a breath. Another. *Stay calm. You've just asked for the Lord's forgiveness; now, all you have to do is hold it together. Don't think about her. Don't think about her. Don't. Think. About. Her.* "About her." I suck in a breath, attempting to retract the words that slipped out, then curl my fingers into fists.

"So," Saint drawls, "you are in a quandary about her."

"I said I'm not in any quandary about her."

"But you actually...are," Damian frowns, "in a quandary about her?"

"Not about her." I scowl.

"Yes, about her." Weston smirks.

"All about her?" Arpad offers.

"No," I square my shoulders, "not at all."

"Yes," Sinner insists, "you are."

Anger thrums at the base of my spine; heat flushes the back of my neck. "It's. Not. About her," I grate out. "It's about me, and the fact that I haven't been able to live up to my vows, my promises, the word I gave to the most important presence in my life when I set upon this path. I haven't been able to adhere to them. Do you understand how that feels? To have your entire world turned upside down in a matter of seconds?" I glance about the room, take in each of their faces in turn. "To look at yourself in the mirror and realize that everything that you've stood for so far was a lie. That the only thing that mattered, the one thing that you thought you could rely on—yourself, your honor, your ability to be truthful to yourself? It's all gone. That you were fooling yourself so far. That you thought you'd come a long way in healing yourself, but really, all you've done is hidden behind a mask — which you thought was your true self, but it isn't, not really. For all there is, is you and the wound that never heals. The one that turned you into your worst nightmare. The one you couldn't live with. Yourself."

By the time I finish ranting, I realize I've said too much. I wish I could retract my words. My chest rises and falls. Goosebumps dot my skin. A bead of sweat slides down my temple as I tuck my elbows into my sides. "What am I doing? Apparently, I can't even control my temper." This is what the thought of her does to me. She's crept into the crevasses of my disguise, torn off the mask I'd donned. She's exposed exactly how weak I am at my core. Is this why the Lord sent her to me. To hold up a mirror to my frailties? To reveal just how fragile my relationship with Him is? To tell me that I haven't changed, not really? For beneath it all, I am still the sad and lonely, tortured boy with a past that will never let go of me.

"What bullshit is this?" Sinclair growls. "Stop being so hard on yourself, Ed." He walks over to me, grips my shoulders. "Of all of us, you and Baron were affected the most by what happened at the incident. And yet, neither one of you has never told us the details."

"And I'm not starting now." I shake off his grasp. "I think it's time you guys go."

"Oh, fuck off," Saint snaps.

I glare at him and he glares back.

"No swearing. Not when you are in the house of the Lord."

"What-fucking-ever," he responds.

"Saint," Sinclair warns, "keep it down. The Father's already hurting. You're not making it any better."

"Of course, the Father's upset." He snorts, "He's realizing that he's not perfect. He's one of us. As flawed, as fallible, as prone to falling in—"

"Stop," I growl. "Don't go there."

"Oh?" Saint tilts his head, "What are you going to do, Ed? You going to punch me in the face? You going to finally give in to the insecurities that crawl inside of you as much as the rest of us? You going to finally get your head out of your arse and do something about your life that's been stalled since the incident?" He takes a step forward and I throw up a hand.

"I'm holding onto my temper with great difficulty here."

"I'm sooo scared." He grins. "What are you going to do about it, Ed? You going to get off your high horse and finally accept that you can't stay separate from reality. That you are like the rest of us. That you're in lust with—"

Something inside of me snaps. My vision narrows; my pores pop. I swipe out and bury my fist in his face. Saint stumbles back as blood spurts from his face. He straightens, shakes his head, then bares his teeth. "Finally," he growls, "fucking finally, you show what's there under that exterior."

"I haven't even started." I take a step forward, swipe out my fist. He ducks, then jumps forward. He lowers his head, charges, catches me in the chest. I hit the ground, Saint on top of me. He raises his fist and I laugh. "Hit me. Go ahead, I deserve this and more."

Saint blinks. He scowls down at me, "What the hell?"

"Why did you stop?" I growl. "Hit me," I command.

"You lost it, man?" He frowns.

"You've lost it." I strike out with my fist and he evades it. Anger seizes me; frustration thrums at my temples. I rear up, smash my forehead into his chin and he yells.

"What the bloody fuck?" He pulls back his fist and I laugh and laugh.

"Do it," I spit out. "Hit me in the face."

He hesitates.

"Or have you lost your nerve?"

Saint's gaze narrows; his nostrils flare. His fist descends toward me. I close my eyes and wait. Wait. The next second, his weight is pulled off of me.

"What the — ?" I snap my eyes open, just as Sinner hauls me to my feet.

Arpad and Damian restrain Saint as he glares at me, chest heaving.

"Stop this." Weston frowns. "You should know better than to rise to the bait, Saint." He turns on me, "And you, Father? What's gotten into you? You taunted him, knowing he was going to lose his temper, and of all the places, in Church."

"The Church?" I blink. "I am in the House of God," I whisper in horror. I squeeze my hands into fists. I've done it. I've sullied the one place that is more holy to me than anywhere else. I've tarnished the most sacred of spaces. I've given in to temptation. Again. What is wrong with me? I hang my head. "Get out of here, all of you," I whisper. "Out."

That's when the ringing of a phone breaks the silence.

Sinclair answers his phone, then glances up at me. "It's for you."

"Me?"

I take the phone from him, "Hello?"

"Edward? It's Isla speaking. I am calling about Ava."

"Ava?" My fingers tighten, "What's wrong with Ava?" My heart begins to race. "Tell me right now."

"She's fine..." Isla hesitates, "but not for much longer."

I hear the sound of music in the background, then something crashes to the floor. A man swears in the background. There's the sound of cheering, then Isla gasps.

"Isla, what's happening?" I frown.

"We are at the National Portrait Gallery bar. You'd better get here fast."

I toss the phone back at Sinner, turn and race for the door, when he calls out, "Better change out of your priestly garb first, Father."

I pause to stare down at myself. Should I take it off? No way, am I going to a bar dressed like this... And yet... Why does it seem like I am making some kind of choice? Does it mean that I am forsaking

Him? No. Of course, not. All I'm doing is going to help out a friend. That's allowed, right?

I shrug off the priest's robes, drape them over the nearest chair.

"Here!" Damian calls out behind me.

I turn and snatch my phone that he tosses in my direction. Then I grab my wallet and keys, and I run for the door.

# 11

*"I love my mum to bits, but she annoys me to no end by agreeing with my Father on most things. Gah! I have come to realize it's really important to stand up for yourself and in what you believe in and not allow a man to dictate how you're going to live your life."*
-From Ava's diary

Ava

"Ava, are you listening? Ava?" I pull the phone away from my shoulder, and stare at it. Raisa called me when I was at the bar, and I stepped out to take her call, and now I regret it. She's reminding me to come to my father's wedding... My father's wedding. OMG, how can those two words even go together? Can I actually look on while he marries someone else? Someone who'll take the place of my mother at his side?

"Ava?" I hear my sister's voice over the phone, and sigh, then press the device to my ear, "I am here, Raisa."

"Are you out clubbing?" I can practically see the scolding expression on her face.

"You don't have to sound so judgmental." I huff.

"I'm not," she protests, "I was just wondering where you were out. That's all."

"Yes, I am at a club, and no, I don't do this every night. I am only out because I've had a few hard days and needed to unwind."

"Of course," she mutters, "must be fun to dance for a living, then also dance to have fun."

"You didn't just say that." I scowl, "Seriously, Raisa. I may not work a desk job like you, but I do have a career... It's just that it's a creative one."

"Of course," Raisa murmurs. Her tone is contrite, but I am not really sure if I believe her. "I am not faulting your career choice, Ava. It's just... I... It's unorthodox, that's all."

*Wait until you hear about my choice in men. Hoo boy, talk about being unorthodox.* I snicker, and all but sense Raisa getting prickly on the other end of the line.

"You don't have to make fun of me," she says in a hurt voice, "I really am trying to understand you, Ava."

"I know you are." I hunch my shoulders. "I know I've been a bitch since Dad broke his news. Well, no, even earlier, since Mom's death..."

There's silence on the line, then I sigh, "Okay, okay. In general, I've been a bit of a brat for a while now."

"Thank you," she exclaims. "Now that we have that out of the way, are you coming to the wedding?"

There's silence. A beat, another. "I... I need to think about it," I finally say.

"Think all you want." Her voice hardens, "Just as long as you come."

We'll see. I am still not sure I want to attend, but if I don't go my dad will be hurt and I don't want that to happen either. *I'll be there,* is what I want to say. Instead, I hold the phone away from my face. "Oh, someone's calling me. I'd better be going. Bye, Raisa."

Coward. I am such a coward. Why is it so difficult to simply tell her that I'll be there? Maybe because it feels like I am being disloyal to Mum if I say that I'll attend the wedding? Despite everything Dad told me, I still don't feel completely right with going to see my Dad marrying another woman. I shake my head. I need to stop obsessing about it and carry on with the reason I am out tonight. Music, dancing. Yes, that's why I came out today, right? To forget all of my worries for a few hours. I pivot, then head for the dance floor.

Twenty minutes later, the music pours over me, ripples down my stomach and in between my legs. I close my eyes, shake my booty, drag my hands up over my head. Let the rhythm infiltrate me, curve around my waist, sizzle down my legs, my toes. Ah. With the right music, the right beats, the right tempo, it's like I am flying. OMG, this is sooo much fun.

I grind my hips, bend my knees, curve my torso to fit to the melody. Swipe my hair up and away from my neck, turn my head to the side, then the other way, grind my hips again, only to brush up against something... Someone. Hands grasp my waist, then I am pulled back and fitted against the unmistakable bulge of male hardness. Warmth grips me. He's here; he came for me. He has to have come. He couldn't stay away. Hot breath grazes my ear, the heat of his body envelops me. The scent of beer and stale sweat assails me. No, not him. Who the hell is this, then? I snap open my eyes as he leans into me.

"Hello baby, wanna go for a test drive?"

Eeeugh. Is that even a pick-up line, or what? I turn around to take in the features of the man who leers down at me. Sweat beads his brow; his cheeks are ruddy. His face boasts a weak chin and his lips are slightly parted as he pants down at me. Just my luck. Of all the creepy crawlies in the world, the grossest of them all had to come onto me. What the hell is wrong with me? Why do I seem to forever attract the wrong kind of man? And the one time I'd been sure my luck was changing, that I'd found someone who was different, and hot and kind and sexy and dominant, and yet, sensitive... Yeah. I know. Turns out, he was too good to be true anyway. "Get away from me."

I try to pull away, but he applies more pressure on my hips and holds me in place. "Now, now," his features brighten, "is that anyway to treat our new-found friendship."

"You're right," I nod, "I'd rather see your head on a spike."

"What?" He blinks.

"No, actually," I press a finger to my cheek, "I think I'd rather dig your heart out and eat it. Better still, bury my fangs in your neck and draw out your blood."

He pales. "Wh...what does that mean?"

"Don't you know?" I lean in close enough for his horrid body odor to overpower me. Ugh, someone get me a bucket. I bare my teeth, "I am a vampire in disguise."

He stares, then bursts out laughing. "You're funny."

"You're not." I pull back my fist, bury it in his throat.

He roars, releases me. I scramble away, lunge forward through the crowd of dancing people. A woman steps in my path; I shove past her. A man dances his way across my progress; I dig my elbow into his side. He yelps, moves away. I dart past, make it to the edge of the dance floor when a heavy hand descends on my shoulder. I yelp, turn and swing. The sweaty barnacle ducks, then tightens his grip with so much force that pain sears my arm.

"Let go of me," I grit through clenched teeth.

"Says you and which army?" He smirks.

"Says me."

I hear the growled-out words, despite the fact that music is booming all around me. Hell, I'd hear him even if he didn't speak. All he'd have to do is think it, and I'll bet I could glean it from his mind... Whoa, hold on. He's not that Edward...and you're not Bella, much as you'd like to be. And this is not a fairytale, or a stalker vampire romance... This...is real life, and he's a priest, and you are a...foolish woman who's developed feelings for him. I twist my shoulder, try to get away again. This time, he hauls me around and against him.

I grimace, "Let me the hell go, you asshole." I dig my elbow back and into his side. He doesn't even lose a breath. He winds his arm around my neck, begins to sway with me. That unwashed body scent of his crowds me and his oily heat crawls around me. Gross. I raise my foot and bring it down on his massive one. He yells, shoves me away from him and straight at Edward, who grabs me, shoves me behind him.

Whoa, okay, not expected. Not that I didn't think he had it in him. I mean, of course, I'd suspected that the priest's facade only partially obscures the over-the-top possessive man hiding somewhere in there. Only, I hadn't been sure. I'd thought he'd saved that part of himself— that crazy devotion that comes from being fixated with something or someone. I'd been sure he was saving all those emotions for the One Above.

So, to have him throw a punch, catch the other guy at the temple and follow that up with a punch to the stomach... All in one move... Whoa... It's hot. Okay, it's crazily hot. I watch, open mouthed, as he follows up with a third hit to the chin. The other guy sways, then crumples to the ground. People move away, give him space, then turn away and continue dancing.

Edward turns on me, his gaze intense. His jaw flexes and a vein throbs at his temple.

"Edward, I—"

He holds up a hand, then jerks his chin toward the exit. I stiffen and he glares at me. Anger thrums from him—vital, real. A dense cloud of heat wafts off of him, slams into my chest. I swallow. Oh, shit. This isn't good. Not at all. He takes a step forward; I scramble back. He moves in my direction. I turn, elbow my way through the crowd, reach the exit, and walk up through the winding staircase, past couples making out, past another couple dry-humping, their tongues down each other's throats. I swallow; my throat goes dry. I turn to glance over my shoulder to find his gaze locked on me. Goosebumps pop on my skin; my thighs clench. I lose my footing and stumble, only for him to grip my waist and straighten me. The warmth of his palms scalds me through my dress. I shiver, and he looks me up and down. His gaze widens. When he glances back at me, his pupils are dilated, his breathing ragged. Then he sets his jaw, schools all expression from his face. He releases me so quickly that I stumble again. This time I right myself. He tips his chin up again.

"So what? Now you're not talking to me?"

His jaw tics.

"Is this some kind of silent treatment?"

His eyebrows draw down. He folds his arms, stares down at me, down that patrician nose of his. His gaze is so intense, so angry...so helpless. I swallow. "Shit, it's never easy between us, is it?"

He blows out a breath, then pinches the bridge of his nose, nods toward the stairs. "Go on," he growls.

I turn, march up the steps, through the crowd of people around the bar, and out the main door onto the sidewalk. The cold instantly washes over me. My fevered skin seems to sigh in gratitude. I turn my face to the light breeze that blows past, hoping to hide my heated cheeks. Then, just like that, the temperature seems to dip. I shiver, wrap my arms about my waist.

"Where's your coat?" he snaps.

"Inside, with Isla." I turn to brush past him, "Maybe I should get it."

"Leave it," he orders, his voice taut. Tension grips every muscle in his body.

He stalks forward. I watch as he reaches a Harley parked a little up the road. He opens the storage box on the bike, pulls out a helmet, then turns to glower at me. What's his problem anyway? And since when do hot, sexy priests drive hot, sexy bikes? Why is it that he's hellbent on breaking every single stereotype I have in my head about men of the cloth? Not that I've known any of them before, considering I haven't ever been to church. What? My parents were agnostic. When they were not too busy quarreling, they were too busy making up. Which left me to my own devices. Hence—the overactive imagination. None of which has ever dared me to dream of this hot as f guy who crooks his finger.

What the hell? Does he think he calls and I'll go running to him? I fold my arms across my chest.

He glares at me and I shiver. It's the wind; that's all it is.

He tilts his head. I tip up my chin. He arches an eyebrow and moisture beads between my legs. He holds out the helmet to me. I draw in a breath, take a step forward, another. By the time I reach him, I am shaking all over. Why does this man affect me so? What is it about him that makes me feel like I am back in high school and in the presence of my biggest ever crush? Umm, maybe because he is? Only it's more than a crush I feel... It's lust...love...? Nah, not that. Ridiculous. How could I be in 'anything' with this man whom I barely know at all?

*But you do... You know enough about him. You know that he's sensitive, that he wants to dedicate himself to a bigger cause, that he wants to help his people, that he wants to remain loyal to his vows, to stay faithful to his one true love.* And how could that not impress me? Strangely, it's the very things that make him unobtainable to me which also make him irresistible. And that, folks, neatly sums up the contradiction that my life often ties itself up in.

He places the helmet on my head. I peer up at him as he pushes the hair away from my neck, before snapping the strap under my chin. His fingertips brush my skin and a shiver races down my back.

He frowns, then pulls out a jacket, drapes it over my shoulders.

"What about you."

"I'm good," he mutters. "Besides, considering you're not wearing much, you need this more than I do."

"I'm wearing enough," I huff as I shove my arms through the sleeves.

"Is that what you call...this...this...bandage that you are swaddled in?" He rakes his gaze down the dress that hits somewhere above my knees.

So, it's a little tight, a little figure hugging, and maybe it emphasizes my boobs and the curve of my arse... But really, it's perfectly respectable. *Side note—yes, I had sorta hoped he'd end up in the bar.* Speaking of... "How did you know where I was?" I frown.

"Isla called Sinclair who handed the phone over to me."

"Oh, wow." I blink. "That's certainly a circuitous route to have taken for you to get to me."

"There are easier ways to get my attention," he grumbles.

"I wasn't trying to get your attention," I retort.

"Weren't you?"

"Of course, not," I lie. "I was merely out on the town, single and footloose, and ready to take someone home tonight—"

"Is that what you were trying to do in there?" He draws himself up to his full height, "Seemed to me, you were trying to get away from that man's unwanted advances."

"I was managing myself well enough, until you came along."

His lips twist, "I am the last person you should be lying to, Eve."

*Don't say it. Don't remind him. Don't, Ava.* "Because you are a priest?"

His jaw tightens. That familiar polite mask—the one I hate, the one that implies that he's hiding away the man behind the persona—is back on his face. Well, too bad. After all, he's made it clear that there can be no relationship between us. So, he can hardly blame me for throwing that at him. And I didn't throw it, as such. I mean, he is a priest. It's his chosen vocation, so why the hell is he so pissed off with me now?

He turns away, straddles the bike, then starts the engine. The boom-boom-boom of the pipes fills the space.

He glances at me sideways. "Get on," he snaps.

I pull the jacket closer. The scent of him floods me and it feels like I am wearing him on myself. If this is the only way I'm going to get close to him, then so be it. I'll take every opportunity I can to spend time with him. I throw my leg over and mount the steed.

He turns and asks, "You, okay?"

I nod.

"Hold on."

I slide in closer, place my hands on his waist. He zooms forward. I yell, then throw my arms around him as he accelerates. The front of my thighs and my chest are flush against him as he whizzes up the road. The cold air buffets my uncovered legs. I huddle even closer to the warmth that emanates from him. And for all that, he isn't wearing a jacket, but he shows no signs of feeling the chill. He really has extra-hot blood. That must be why he's also such a smokin' hottie. I snicker against his back, and the muscles under his skin seem to ripple. The only thing separating me from him is my jacket and the thin shirt that he's wearing. If I slipped my hand in between the plackets, I'd finally be able to touch, sense, feel what it means to be skin to skin with him.

Liquid heat pools in my core. My mouth waters. I turn my face into his shirt, draw from it deeply. The scent that is pure Edward overpowers my senses, and just like that, I am wet. Maybe I should bottle it. That way, when he's not around, I can still sniff him. Hell, I could come just by touching myself as I smell him. *Gah! Stop that...*

He turns off the main road and I glance around me. Huh? This is not the way to my place, so where are we going? Is he taking me to his... Where does he live? Near the church? He can't be taking me there...surely?

He turns off again, under a bridge, then around another round-about, turns to the right, and there, in front of us, is the Tower Bridge, otherwise known as London Bridge, but from an angle I've never seen it.

We seem to be almost under it, but not quite. The entire structure is lit up in a silvery light that turns it into a beautiful artefact that is ageless, timeless... So serene that it's almost tranquil, despite the hustle and bustle of the city. How many others have watched it from exactly this angle? Who were they? What did they do? Did they also come here because they were avoiding something...like the big elephant between us...aka this attraction, this connection...this... completely insane need to be close to him, to feel him, touch him, hear him speak, laugh, to kiss his eyelids, his mouth, his cheeks, that beautiful throat of his that flexes when he's angry and stretches when he's sad. I swallow as he pulls over by a small park. He shuts off the bike and silence descends. My heart begins to thud and my pulse pounds at my temples. Why did he bring me here? To talk? About what?

Why isn't he saying anything yet?

I slide off the bike, pull the jacket even closer. He lowers the kick-stand, disembarks, then opens the storage box on the bike. He pulls out a pair of leather pants and hands them to me. "Put them on; you're cold," he commands.

I grimace. "Is this how you speak to your flock? Do you order them around as well?"

A nerve throbs at his temple. "I didn't bring you here to argue with you."

"Then why did you bring me?"

He rolls his shoulders. "Come." He gestures me toward the park.

I step into the pants, fold up the hems so I don't trip on them. The waist band is elastic and I fold it a few times until it perches on my hips. Not very comfortable, but it'll keep me warm.

I cross the sidewalk, and head up the small park to a bench that faces the view of the bridge.

I sink down and he sits… As far away from me as possible on the other side of the space.

My heart deflates a little. Shit, what was I expecting? That we'd hold hands and gaze into each other's eyes. As if. I stare ahead at the piece of marvelous architecture that stands there as if suspended in the darkness.

For a few seconds we don't speak. My muscles unwind and I slide down the bench a little. The cold sinks into my blood and I stamp my feet to stay warm. "If only there was something warm to drink," I mutter aloud, then blink when he slides a flask across the space.

I shoot him a sideways glance. "What's that?"

"Whiskey."

"I didn't know you drank."

"There's a lot you don't know about me."

"Only because you don't share anything with me."

He opens his mouth and I hold up my hand, "I know, I know, it's not like we've had much time to get to know one another; still..." I shuffle my feet, "all I'm saying is that I'd like to find out more about you."

He blows out a breath, then leans forward. "What do you want to know?"

# 12

Edward

What the hell am I doing? Clearly, I have lost it. That's the explanation for why I brought her here...to my secret spot. The place I've been coming to on my own since I was young. Staring at that incredible piece of manmade wonder is a reminder that there is hope. That if man puts his mind to it, he can overcome insurmountable challenges. That I can, perhaps, despite my past, try to break free and embrace who I have become. If only it were that easy to figure out what to do about this...whatever it is, between us. And, yes there is a connection here... I could turn a blind eye to it, I could try to avoid it, and that's what I've been doing, but my reaction to finding out that she was in trouble...had thrown me. I hadn't been able to stop myself from going to her, putting myself between her and the bastard who had tried to physically touch her... He'd...he'd...put his hands on her and I'd lost it. At that moment, nothing else mattered except teaching him a lesson. That he couldn't touch what was mine. That no one else could

come near what belongs to me. That she... Belongs to me. That she...
Is mine.

"Fuck." I rub my palm across my face.

Next to me she goes completely still. "Did you just—?"

"Swear?" I laugh bitterly. "That's the least of my sins."

"Have you sinned, Father?"

I stiffen, then turn to her. "I am sitting here with you, aren't I?"

She tilts her head, "Are you saying I make you sin?"

"What do you think?"

"I think," she turns to stare ahead, "that you can do anything you
want, you can be anything you choose to be, but you've put barriers
around yourself and you hold yourself up to impossibly high stan-
dards, the kind most men would find it difficult to live up to and—"
She swallows. "That only makes you even more desirable."

"Where did you learn to speak like that?"

"Like what?"

"Like you are laying out all of your emotions to the world and not
hiding a thing." I shoot her a sideways glance. "Don't you have any
self-preservation?"

"Not where you are concerned."

"You're not making this easy." I curl my fingers into fists. "I should
leave you and walk away from here."

"Why don't you?"

"I should turn around and get out of your sight and never come
near you again." I set my jaw.

"Do you really want to do that?"

"I should let you lead a life far, far away from me." I roll my
shoulders.

"Will you be able to do that?"

"No," I lower my chin, "and that is the problem."

"What are you trying to say, Father?"

"That I have taken my vows, I am bound to the Church, and I will
never be available for you as a man is for a woman."

"And yet, you came to the bar, knowing I was there, then proceeded
to step in between me and another man, then drive me on your bike—

which, by the way, was totally unexpected — and, bring me here..." She nods to the glorious sight of the illuminated bridge in front of us. "A place that is clearly special to you, so pardon me for feeling confused."

"I brought you here so I could get to know you."

"But you just said —"

I raise my hand, "Let me complete the statement. To get to know you as a friend."

"As a friend?"

"That's what we agreed to earlier, right?" I tilt my head.

"Hmm, the way you burst in on me at the bar, Father, I could have sworn you were jealous."

"Edward," I snap. "Call me Edward when it's just the two of us."

"Edward." She rolls the word about her tongue as if testing it, and every one of my senses focuses in on her. The sound of my name from her lips sends my pulse racing. This won't do. I am sitting here, hoping to come to terms with what can't be. Trying to find a way forward, but it seems everything I do only connives to deepen the attraction between us.

"And I wasn't jealous," I insist. "I merely saw that the guy was bothering you at the bar and did what anyone else in my position would have done.

"But no-one else came to help me; only you did," she points out.

"Guess, my reflexes were quicker than theirs, hmm?"

"Is that what you're telling yourself?" she mutters.

"It's true, though." I set my jaw. "And I forbid you from ever going to a bar again dressed like that."

"Dressed like what?" She glances down at herself. "I'm wearing a perfectly decent dress."

"A dress that's so short it barely covers your crotch."

"It comes to mid-thigh."

"Too short."

"It's what I'd wear during the day when I'm not dancing."

"Change your wardrobe."

Her jaw drops. "How dare you?" She springs up to her feet. "First, you tell me there can't be anything between us. Then, you think you can dictate what I should and shouldn't wear. If I didn't know better, I'd think that you were my—"

"What?"

"Father."

*Ouch.* I set my jaw. "I am merely a concerned friend."

"Oh?" She snorts. "And what are you concerned about?"

"Your safety, of course."

"So, if I decided to date other men, that'd be fine?"

My guts twist and anger laces my blood. I stare ahead, jerk my chin.

"And if I decided to sleep with someone else, you'd be okay with that?"

I dig my fingernails into the palm of my hand and squeeze down with such force that pain lances up my arm. I nod my head.

"Will you?" she asks.

I school all emotion from my face, turn to her. "Yes," I force the word through a throat gone dry. "Yes, I would."

Her features distort, a tear runs down her cheek, and a hot sensation stabs at my chest. I reach for her, but she steps away. She turns her back to me, and the cold seems to intensify.

"I'm glad we cleared this up, *Father*." She stares ahead.

"Edward—" I correct her, "I told you to call me Edward."

"I'd prefer to stick to the right title, considering there can't be anything more between us." She squares her shoulders, "I'd better be getting home."

She pivots and begins to walk away.

I jump up, follow her, "I'll take you."

"No, thanks." She speeds up. I easily overtake her, plant myself in her path, and she pauses. " Get out of my way." Her voice waivers. She lowers her face so her thick hair obscures her features.

"Ava, please." I reach for her, but she steps aside.

"Don't touch me," she beseeches me. "Please." She starts walking again and I follow her. Is she crying? Did I do that? Did I upset her? My chest tightens. Of course, I upset her. Every time I meet her, I upset her, and yet I can't stay away from her.

She reaches my bike, walks by it. "Ava, stop." I race forward, step in her path once more. She comes to a stop, but keeps her head bowed.

"Look at me."

She shakes her head.

"Don't disobey me," I snap, and she jerks her head up. Tears glisten on her cheeks; her eyes flash green fire at me.

"There, happy?" she snarls. "You wanted to see how your words affect me? You wanted to ensure that I am heartbroken by what you told me, that you broke up with me?" She pushes her finger into her cheek. "Oh, wait! Of course, not. How could we break up, considering we had no relationship to speak of? And we don't, do we? Have a relationship?"

I rake my gaze across her features, the flushed cheeks, the parted lips, her jutted out chin that hints at the stubbornness in her—something I am already well acquainted with.

"Ava," I reach for her, then withdraw my hand. "You're wrong. We have a connection, something that is unique and will always bind us together. But I can't act on it. You understand that, right?"

"I do, but do you?" She swallows. "Perhaps that's why you feel the need to continuously run into me? So, you can tell yourself that there can't be anything between us. And yet, you keep finding excuses to come to me."

I purse my lips. "That won't happen again."

Her lower lip trembles, her eyes fill with fresh tears, her shoulders shudder, and help me, God, but I can't stop myself. I pull her to me, and wrap my arms around her. "I'm sorry, I truly am. I wish I could do something about this situation, but I can't."

"You can." She sniffles. "You can leave the Church."

I stiffen. "That's not going to happen; I take my vows seriously. When everything else around me was collapsing, the Church was there for me. I found solace in The Lord. He's the reason I was able to go on with my life and why I am standing here today. I can't abandon Him at the first instance I face a crisis of faith."

"Is that what you think I am?" She pulls back in the circle of my arms, "A crisis?"

"You are—" I peer into those beautiful green eyes of hers, "the most beautiful, most gorgeous, most loving woman I have ever met. Your passion for what you do, the intensity with which you live every moment, your sheer vivacity is unparalleled, Ava. You deserve someone better than me. Someone who can give you everything you desire."

"I want you."

"I am not yours to have."

She tries to pull away, but I tighten my hold on her. "No, don't leave, please just listen to me."

She huffs, then stills in my arms. "What is it?" she mumbles under her breath. "What do you want to tell me?"

"I'll never forget you, Ava. Never forget how you smile, how you laugh with your entire spirit, how when you're angry about something, your eyes flash. How when you dance, you put your entire mind and body and soul into it. You become one with the rhythm, Ava, and if that isn't true worship, I don't know what is."

She stares up into my face. "I... I don't understand," she whispers. "What are you trying to tell me?"

"I thought I could be friends with you. God knows, I've tried. But I underestimated the intensity of the chemistry between us. Clearly, I am not strong enough to resist it." My throat closes. I swallow down the ball of emotions, then peer into her eyes. "Try to understand, what I am doing is for the best."

She shakes her head, "No, no, please don't."

"I won't try to see you again. I won't approach you. I'll let you go so you may live your life to the fullest, only..." I squeeze my eyes shut, "only I won't be there to see it."

"Don't do this, Edward," she implores me. "You're not even giving us a chance."

"I am giving you the best possible chance at living."

"I'll die without you."

I half smile. "No, you won't. You'll survive, you'll thrive, you'll embrace your dreams, fulfill your destiny. You'll become a well-known dancer, a devoted wife, the kind of mother every child should have." Pain twists my insides and my breath catches. I hunch my shoulders, force myself to step back from her.

She closes the space between us, launches herself at me. "I won't let you go. I won't let you do this to us."

"It's done." I should push her away, keep distance between us, but as she tilts her chin up, I find I don't have the strength. I pull her close, wind my arms about her, hold her as if I'll never get the chance again... Which I won't.

She holds my gaze and her features pale. A teardrop rolls down her cheek, and I bend down, then lick it up.

She stills. "Why did you do that?"

I swallow down the salty taste, then release her again. "So, I'll always have you with me."

"You have my heart, Edward."

"No, I don't." I take a step away from her. "You must keep it safe with you, Ava, so you can give it to a man who deserves it more than me."

# 13

Ava

That had been two days ago. Forty-eight hours. A lifetime. After that little bombshell he'd dropped on me, Edward had insisted on dropping me back home. I hadn't protested. Maybe I'd been too numb from the finality of his words. He'd meant it. I'd gazed into his eyes and the look in them had indicated that this time he was going to walk away. He wasn't going to return and tell me he wanted to try to be friends. Well, we'd tried that and look how well that had gone? I should respect his wishes, let him get back to what is important to him. His Church, his vows, his God.

Does God not have enough people worshipping Him, that He also has to bind my Edward to Him? Why can't He let Edward go? Would it help if I prayed to Him? The last time I'd prayed was when my mother had been unwell. Not that it had helped much.

But if Edward believes in Him so much, does that mean I could appeal to Him to release him? Would God actually hear me?

It hadn't helped before, but given how hopeless everything feels now, it couldn't hurt to start, right?

Which is why, after finishing my dance class for the day, I've walked into the nearest church. The temperature instantly dips and goosebumps rise on my skin. I slide my hands into my coat and walk up the aisle. It's late afternoon, and the sun's rays slant through the stained-glass windows that line the walls on either side of the aisle. I take a pew a couple of rows from the front, then kneel down and place my elbows on the back of the seat in front of me. Ahead of me is the altar, and beyond that, the statue of Christ on the cross. I fold my fingers together, bend my head and studiously avoid looking at Him. After all, it's His fault I'm here. He's the reason I can't get Edward to consider anything beyond a platonic relationship... And not even that. Any kind of connection, really... It's because He has Edward's loyalty that I have no place in his life. I squeeze my eyes shut. Hell... No... Sorry, no swearing. Let's start again.

*Dear God, I am not a regular church goer but I am here because... Well, I really don't have the right to ask You this. I mean, I know it's probably forbidden to even think about him that way. The 'him' here refers to Edward, of course. Funny how it's easy to refer to him as Edward and not Father. Truth be told, I never could get used to calling him Father. I couldn't really regard him as a 'Father,' if you know what I mean? Now you, God... You, I'd call Father. Because, well, you are the Father of all of us. I'm sorry I haven't come in and prayed to You before... I've just been busy with this business of growing up and figuring out how to make something of myself, know what I mean?*

*But I am here now...and hmm... Come to think of it, is that why You made me meet Edward?* One way of bringing me to Your doorstep? I bite down on my lower lip. *It couldn't be, could it? This isn't all some crazy convoluted plan for the One Above to remind me to pray, is it?*

*Though, if it is, then You've succeeded, for I am here on my knees, begging You to help me.*

*Asking You if there is any chance in hell—okay not hell, forget I said that—just a chance, really, that You'd consider giving me and him an opportunity to be together, because, you know, since I saw him, since I laid eyes on him, my world has changed. I mean, I hadn't even been aware of what I had been waiting for until I saw him... Does that make sense? He came into my life and I knew then… It's him. The one I'd hoped to find some day. My other half. He grounds me, God, he…makes me believe anything is possible. Much like You do. When I am here and praying to You, I can focus on what is possible. On the future, on what is to come, and things I didn't even know I wanted. It's like I am on the verge of something momentous that's about to take place. Or maybe it is the sense of possibilities that has my heart racing?*

*That sense of calm, yet the prickle of excitement from knowing that You can make anything happen…that adrenaline that laces my blood, that sensation of the infinite, that I am but a speck of sand in time, and really, that my concerns are so minuscule in comparison to the wider plan… And there is a plan in store for me. There is…the one that You're unfolding. I can't see it… but I believe in it. Just as I believe in him. Despite everything I do, I am confident that there will be a chance for us to be together… I just have to trust.*

Can I trust?

Can I?

My head spins, I snap my eyes open, glance up at Him on the cross. A strange stillness fills me. The hair on the back of my neck rises. My heart begins to race and my pulse rate speeds up. It's as if I am on the precipice of something…something… That all of this was orchestrated and I am but the pawn in a design that I cannot yet see fully. "Is that true?" I whisper. "Should I believe in You? In him? Is that why You brought me here? Will everything work out?"

I hear the susurration of wings, a white pigeon—or is that a dove —? flies down from the ceiling. It alights on the cross, and its guttural cooing echoes through the space. Goosebumps pop on my skin. Oh, my… That's…that's a sign. It has to be, right?

The dove cocks its head to the left, then the right, before flying up toward the ceiling. It heads for the open door and I follow it. I reach the door, step out. I follow the bird down the steps, across the sidewalk. I watch as it flares out its wings to soar up, and further up. I take a step forward, miss the curb and stumble and fall onto the road.

A car horn sounds and I glance up, straight into the path of an oncoming vehicle.

My heart begins to race, the pulse pounds at my temples, and sweat beads my forehead. I throw up my palms to shield myself and

squeeze my eyes shut, only to be hauled to my feet and back onto the
sidewalk.

The car horn blares as the vehicle speeds by, and I am yanked
against a hard, firm, broad chest. The scent of fresh cut grass teases
my nostrils. My heart hammers so hard, I am sure it's going to break
out of my chest. Bands of steel seem to tighten around me as he tucks
me into him, one arm about my shoulders, the other across my back
and waist as he pivots away from the curb.

How the hell had he moved that fast? Where had he come from?
How did he know that I was in danger? Are we forever doomed to be
connected somehow, no matter how we might try to wrench ourselves
away from each other?

"What the hell were you thinking?" he growls as he turns me to
face him.

"The...the dove..." I stutter.

"Dove?" he frowns.

"I followed it out from the church. The next thing I knew, I was
falling forward...and...and —" A sob wells up, and he pulls me closer.

"Shh! It's okay, I've got you. I have you; nothing can harm you
now."

The sound of his voice through me, sinks into my blood. My
nipples tighten — is it because of his nearness, or the near miss with
the car, or both, perhaps? I try to answer but my throat is too dry. My
limbs tremble and my knees knock together. I push my nose into the
valley that demarcates his pecs, dig my fingers into the front of his
shirt, and hold on as he swings me up into his arms, with my handbag
crushed between us.

I glance up, past the white of the collar at his neck, to the thrust of
his pouty lower lip, that mean upper lip, the bead of sweat that slides
down the sinews of his throat. Heat flushes my skin and my stomach
flip-flops. Every part of me is alert and alive, and so in awe of where I
am. *In his arms, being carried by him.*

He enters the church, walks up the aisle, all the way up to the
altar, before turning and heading toward a door on the left. He walks
through what looks like an office — because of the large desk in a
center — out through another door in the back, down a garden path,

with flower beds on each side, to a small one-story Victorian structure built from red bricks with a slate roof. He walks up the steps, shoulders the door open and steps inside. He carries me to the couch, and lays me down, setting my head on a throw pillow.

I sit up and he points a finger at me. "Stay," he snaps.

"But," I swallow, "Edward, I—"

"Not a word." He glares at me and I shiver. My thighs clench and moisture gathers between my legs. Shit, why the hell do I find his dominant manner so hot?

He walks inside a door which I assume leads to his bedroom. My handbag slides from my arm to the floor. I slump back in the couch, swallow down the thickness that clogs my throat. That was close, like, really, really close... If Edward had been one second too late, if I had lurched forward a second earlier... If the car had been speeding even a little faster.... I gulp. My limbs tremble. Shivers ripple up my spine and I wrap my arms around my waist to stay warm.

"Here." His voice interrupts my thoughts, and I snap my eyelids open. He drops a cover over me, tucks it in under my chin. "Scoot over," he mutters.

I scoot in further and he sinks down next to me. He places a first-aid kit on the table, then opens it and pulls out some cotton and antiseptic. He takes my hand in his, turns my arm, pushes up the sleeve of my dress and dabs at the gash I only now notice. Pinpricks of pain spark at my nerve-endings, and another bout of shaking grips me.

"You okay?" He frowns.

"Y...yes." I say through chattering teeth. "D...don't know what's wrong."

"Delayed reaction," he reassures me as he continues to dab at the injured skin. He rips a packet open, pulls out the bandage and places it over the scrape. He takes my palm, turns it face up.

"Wh... what are you doing?" I whisper.

He doesn't respond. Simply pours out more antiseptic onto the cotton ball, then proceeds to dab it on my palm where the skin has abraded. I wince. Again, I hadn't noticed it.

Guess I'd been too caught up in what was happening in the

moment to realize I'd banged myself up. Another few seconds, and I might not be here on Edward's sofa in his house.

OMG, I am in his house, on his couch, and he's taking care of me. It's what I wanted, right? So why am I so close to tears? Besides, I didn't die. I am still here. I am alive and near him.

My entire body shudders and he frowns, then rises to his feet. He heads for a wooden cabinet in the corner, pulls out a bottle, and pours some of the liquid into a glass. When he returns, he sits down next to me again. He slides an arm under my neck, raises my head, and holds the glass to my lips. I stare into his handsome features. Those dark eyebrows, thick eyelashes, his dark hair messed up and falling over his forehead. He looks a little shaken, not as put together as all the times I've seen him in the past.

He jerks his chin at me, "Drink."

I take a sip and the alcohol burns its way down my throat. My stomach is suddenly on fire and I gasp. Tears prick my eyes and I blink them away.

"Again," he orders.

I hold his gaze, stare into those bright, beautiful eyes of his which glare at me with so much emotion that I gulp. He frowns, nods again to the glass, and I take another sip. This one goes down smoother. Warmth creeps under my skin; my breathing grows more ragged.

I wrap my fingers over where he holds the glass, and goosebumps rise on my skin.

His throat moves as he swallows and his gaze intensifies further. I take another sip, and another. I swallow down the liquid as heat permeates my cheeks, my chest, snakes down further. I squeeze my thighs together.

His nostrils flare. Those golden irises dilate. He stands abruptly, tosses back the remaining alcohol.

Then he walks back to the cabinet, pours another healthy dose of the whiskey, and tosses it back. Whoa. Are priests allowed to drink? Guess they are. I mean, they do drink wine during Communion, right? And why would he have whiskey in his house if he can't drink?

I take in his tall figure; the broad shoulders clad in his customary black shirt tucked into black pants. The fabric molds to his slim hips,

and clings to those powerful thighs. He's not wearing his robe...
Guess I caught him off-duty. Of all the churches in all the world, I
had to walk into this one. I snicker to myself. What I wouldn't give to
meet him in a gin joint instead.

He jerks, as if the sound cut through his thoughts. He places the
glass back on one of the shelves of the cabinet, then turns to me, "We
need to talk."

# 14

Edward

She watches me with those big green eyes that seem to have swallowed up her face. Her features are drawn, there are shadows under her eyes, and her cheekbones seem too prominent. Has she lost weight since I last saw her? I frown, take a step toward her, then stop. *What are you going to do? Are you going to go back to her? Sit next to her, take her hand in yours, place your palm against her cheek and feel the softness of her skin, draw in the sweet scent of jasmine that clings to her hair?* I clasp my hands behind my back, then begin to pace. Back, forth, back.

She clears her throat, "Edward?"

I continue to pace.

"Ed? Please stop, you're making me dizzy."

I pause, then pivot around and stalk over to her. I stand over her, rake my gaze down her face. "What the hell is wrong with you?" I snap. "You walked out onto that road without a modicum of self-preservation. What were you thinking, Ava?"

She pales further. Her lips tremble, and she presses them together. "Edward, I, I..."

I hold up a hand, "No, don't tell me. You came here to get my attention, didn't you? You decided that since I wasn't interested in you, you'd try a different tactic this time? You walked out there, knowing I would come after you and save you. Well, guess what? I won't be there every time, Ava. The next time you try something so completely stupid, I may not be around to help."

Anger twists my guts; the band around my chest tightens. My knees tremble, and I squat down to disguise just how unable my legs are to support my weight right now.

"What do you have to say for yourself, huh? Do you deny that you purposely placed yourself in the path of that bloody car?"

She blinks. "Wow, that's twice."

"Twice what?"

"Twice that you swore in the last two minutes."

I drag my fingers through my hair. "Is that all you registered from what I told you?"

"Umm, no. You also mentioned that you're not interested in me, and that's incorrect."

I glare at her. "And what else?"

"That I placed myself in the path of that bloody vehicle—"

Anger thuds at my temples. If anything had happened to her... If she'd been hit... If she'd been hurt, or worse... What would I have done? Not all the prayers in the world would have brought her back then.

I glare at her and she swallows. "I didn't, Edward. I didn't step in front of that car on purpose. It was an accident. I told you so already."

Of course, I know that. Ava's artistic and sometimes preoccupied with her thoughts. That doesn't mean she's going to willfully put herself in the path of harm... I'd followed her out of the church, my feet seeming to have a will of their own, but had stopped myself from going to her. Then, I'd seen her pitch forward, that car speeding toward her... I'd lost it. I'd raced for her, had not even been aware how my feet had touched the ground. I'd reached her, pulled her up out of harm's way and then... I couldn't let go of her.

I can't let go of her. I must. I have to. But what if I can't? What then?

"Edward?" She places her palm against my cheek, "Look at me, Ed."

"Ava." I swallow down the ball of emotion that clogs my throat. "Ava." I turn my face into her palm and kiss it, the softness of her skin, a caress. She cups my cheek, turns my face toward her.

I stare into those green eyes, the eyes of an angel, the gaze of a temptress, the fire that burns in them, my fate.

I rub my thumb across her lower lip. She flicks out her tongue and licks it. The blood empties to my groin and all of my senses focus on her. I lean in, capture her mouth with mine.

She parts her lips and I sweep my tongue inside, swipe it across her teeth, suck on her tongue, press my lips to hers, tilt my head and deepen the kiss.

She moans low in her throat and the sound sweeps through my mind. My muscles tense; my belly hardens. I tear my mouth from hers, peer into her face.

*I can't do this.*

*You must.*

*I can't betray my faith.*

*You have no choice.*

*Is this Your way of testing me again, my Lord? Is this how You take me to the edge, only to thrust me over and over again into the path of this sin? Do You want me to embrace it? Is that why You'd put her in the path of danger? To show me just how powerless I am in front of Your will?*

*I'd thought myself infallible...untouchable, unapproachable; getting closer to the perfection that is You...and that was my mistake. So much ego, so much self-confidence, so much conviction in myself... When all along, I had been setting myself up for a fall. I see the error of my ways now, my Lord. I understand the mistake I've made all along. To think I could even attempt to be like You when, really, I am nothing but the dust on Your feet. I've spent all of my life trying to come closer to my ideal of perfection, to come closer to You, when really any attempt at thinking that I could be infallible is wrong.*

*I am, but human and prone to temptation. I may be Your vessel, but my flesh and blood still belong to that of a man. A man driven by his compulsion, the need to be close to her, to take her, embrace her, be with her in all the ways that a man can with a woman.*

*Will You forgive me, my Lord, if I sin?*

*Can I forgive myself if I do?*

*What am I if I do?*

*What am I if not my vows, the ability to hold onto my control, to resist every single temptation thrown in my path? The money has never been of consequence to me. No other woman has ever enticed me like this. As for obedience... What is Your will for me, my Lord? Did You put her in my path because You want me to fail?*

*Do You not want me in Your fold anymore? Am I not a vessel for Your Presence? Do You not want me to serve others in Your name? Is this my time to leave, to find out what lies in store for me outside of Your home?*

My heart begins to thud in my chest. My pulse pounds at my temples. Sweat beads my forehead. I hold her gaze, and perhaps some of my inner turmoil shows, for she pales. I rise to my feet, turn to leave, and she grabs my hand.

"Wait, Father, will you not hear my confession before you leave?"

I frown. "You're not Catholic."

"I can still confess, right?"

"So, you're willing to share your secrets with me?"

She nods.

I scowl. "And what if I use it against you?"

"But you won't." She sits up. Her color is better, her gaze clear. "You'll listen and you'll forgive without judgement because that's what you do, Father."

"You have so much faith in me?"

"Not in you, but in your faith," she replies. "I know when it comes to your profession, you'd never compromise."

"So much trust." I roll my shoulders. "What if I don't live up to it?"

"But you will." She rises to her feet and the blanket falls away. *Don't look there, don't.* I take in the curve of her bust, her nipples pointed and outlined against the fabric of her dress. That familiar ache that has become an ever-present sensation since I first saw her intensifies. My groin hardens. I pivot, walk to the door, when she asks, "Don't you need your outfit?"

I turn and she points to where I've draped the frock over a chair. "Your robe, Father," she prompts me.

I stare at the robe then back at her. "I don't need it to hear your confession. As long as I am ordained—and I am—that is enough."

I head for the door, then pause and glance at her over my shoulder, "Coming?"

# 15

Ava

He's going to leave me. He's going to leave me. He's going to...
leave me and there's nothing I can do about it. He's going to
choose Him over me, as he always does. He's going to leave me
to return to the Church. I know it just by the tormented look in
his eyes. By how he holds my gaze and refuses to look away, how
he steels himself as if waiting for the worst that is yet to come...
which could be possibly, what? What could be more horrible
than him walking away from me a final time, and never looking
back?

I can't let him go.

Not after what just happened. He saved me...metaphorically and
literally; he had rescued me from myself. If I had been ready to walk
away from him earlier, now... I am not. Now, I am going to fight for
him, with every bone in my body. Which is why I'd pulled out the
only trick I have. I'd asked him to hear my confession.

Bugger, bugger, bugger.

I stare at the confessional booth. I haven't been to a confession before, but I've seen enough movies to know how it's done.

He takes his position behind the screen, and I slip into the adjacent cubicle. I kneel, then lock my fingers together; stare through the screen, at the hint of his chin, the angle of his nose, the curve of his beautiful lips that are visible through the lattice work.

"You wanted to confess?" His voice echoes in the enclosed space.

I open my mouth to speak, but my throat is so dry that nothing emerges.

"Ava?" He prompts me, "You said you have something to confess?"

"Y...yes."

Shit, why is it that when I need the powers of conversation most, words fail me? I shuffle my feet, hunch my shoulders, then straighten them. "Um, maybe this was a bad idea. Maybe I shouldn't have suggested it."

"Perhaps your subconscious wants you to open up? Often, speaking what's on your mind is the best way to gain perspective. At the very least, if you talk, it'll shut me up."

"Not that you say a lot," I mutter. "In all the time I've known you, which I admit isn't that long, you've never mentioned anything about yourself."

"This is your confession, not mine," he reminds me.

"You always have a ready answer."

"Not this time. All I'm going to do is listen, without judgement, remember?"

I hear the smirk in his voice. Asshole... Wait, that's not right. You can't call a priest an asshole... However much he is one. Right? And this is Edward, toned down in his role as a priest. How would he be if he weren't one? Why am I even thinking of that, considering that will never be a possibility? It's why I am here, after all, in a confessional, with him in the one role he is comfortable playing.

I blow out a breath, then lower my head,

"You start with saying, 'forgive me, Father, for I have...'"

"Bugger that."

"Eve!" he admonishes me and I subside.

"Do I have to say that?"

"Do you want to confess?"

"Yes. Yes, I do." I lower my chin, "Forgive me, Father, for I have sinned... This is...ah. This will be my first confession."

There's silence from his side, then, "That's all right. Tell me your sins," he commands, and a shiver runs down my spine.

Here goes. "I lied to you."

"About what?"

"About being attracted to you."

"Is that right?"

I nod.

"I am in love with you, Edward,"

There, I've said it. For better or for worse, it is out there now. Maybe it's a low blow to stop him from leaving, but what else do I have in my arsenal, right?

"Did you hear me?" I prompt.

"You haven't known me long enough to have fallen in love with me."

"Just like you have fallen for me; you just haven't allowed yourself to acknowledge it."

"Why do you think you are in love with me?"

I frown. "That sounds more like a psychologist's question than a priest's."

He chuckles. "A good priest is also a psychologist when it matters."

Right.

"So, why do you think you are in love with me?"

"Because I am."

"Answer the question," he snaps.

I stiffen, then choose my words carefully. "Because...before I met you, I didn't know what to do with myself. I loved dancing, but that was it. Anything outside of that? I was no good at it. I didn't know how to live...didn't know what I wanted to wear, what to eat, what to drink, when not to say the wrong thing. I was adrift, unmoored, like I'd been waiting for a signal in the dark, a beacon to guide me, a force to propel me. Something that would take me by my hand and point me in the right direction. Or maybe someone." I tilt my head. "Someone who'd tell me when to get up, what to wear, when to eat, when to sit, when to vote, when to dance, when to relax. Someone who'd take the choices out of my hand and direct me on how to survive. I want someone to believe in me... I want someone like you to guide me, to steer me, to be my conscience, to hear what my soul wants and interpret it for me. Because that's what you do, Father, right? You're the one who advises and directs people. You lead, they follow. That...that's what I want."

There's silence then, "What?" he asks in a low voice. "What is it that you're asking for?"

"Forgiveness for what I am about to ask for, Father."

"What's that?"

"For you to tell me what to do."

"And you'd obey."

"Always, and only for you, Father." I swallow, clench my thighs together. What the hell am I doing? What am I doing? *Don't say it, don't.* "I want you to direct me, to command me, to take control of my life and of me, my choices. I want you to tell me what to do, Father."

Silence extends for a beat, another. He's quiet for so long that I lean forward. I peer through the lattice, but I can't make out his expression. Shit.

I stand up, then press my palm into the screen that separates us.

What the hell is he thinking about? Did I upset him? Have I gone too far? This was a terrible idea. It really was. Why don't you ever know when to shut up, Ava? I turn to head out of the booth, "Edward I—"

"Kneel." His tersely spoken word whispers through the space. I blink.

"Excuse me... What...what did you say?"

"I said, on your knees."

I hesitate. What the hell is he talking about? He surely doesn't mean that, does he?"

"Now," he snaps and I slide onto the floor, on my knees.

# 16

Edward

What the hell am I doing? Why had I agreed to listen to her confession? I should have left right then, though that might have been difficult, considering we were in my house. And no way, would I have asked her to leave, not after that almost accident. Thank God, nothing had happened to her. Thank the Lord, she's on the other side of the screen on her knees. *On. Her. Knees.* My belly hardens. The knot that had gathered there since the day I'd seen her coils even tighter. *It's not too late. You can still leave.* And what? Turn to God again? With what courage?

The one thing He'd asked of me, my loyalty, and I have tarnished it already.

No longer is there space for only Him… Where once He had been my sole focus day and night, there is now another.

As long as I've followed Him, I've never faced a challenge like this one.

Oh, I've had ample opportunity to turn away, to find my way back to the fold. But at every turn, I've come up against her—my feelings of her, my feelings for her, my need...my lust... My love... It is all that, and more. She'd been wrong in saying that I am interested in her. What I feel for her goes far beyond that. It is this shining something inside of her that only I can see. From the moment I'd sensed it, I'd known. And I've been fighting against it. And now, it is too late.

I rise to my feet, walk around to the confessional and pull the curtain aside. I find her kneeling, head lowered. Such a faithful lamb. Such a trusting woman. She is the ultimate Eve. Seductress. Temptress. Innocent and appealing. Lusty and guileless. Naive and wise, at the same time.

I step fully inside the booth, allowing the curtain to close behind me, then gaze down at her bent head.

A growl rips from my throat and she shivers. I lower my hand to her face, pinch her chin, and apply enough pressure for her to peek up at me from between her eyelashes. Her lips part; she gazes into my eyes. Her own shine a bright emerald in the murky light. She swallows, holding my gaze. The scent of her seems to intensify further and heat jolts in my belly. My thighs spasm; my stomach hardens. I reach down, push a strand of her hair behind her ear. She shivers.

"Edward—"

I shake my head, and she subsides.

I drag my finger down her cheek, down the slim column of her neck to the shadowed cleft between her breasts. She shudders, moans deep in her throat. The band around my chest tightens.

*Is this it then? Do you want me to leave the only thing I have ever loved in my life? The safety, the seclusion, the meaning of what life is... You taught me that, and now you are abandoning me?*

"Ed." She reaches out, places a palm on the tent at my crotch and a groan rips out of me.

"You will not move until I give you permission," I hiss.

She pales, retracts her hand, then nods. "As you wish, Father."

A shudder grips me. It shouldn't please me when she calls me that, but it does. How it does. And how damned I am for it. I am going to Hell, no doubt about it. If this is what is intended for me, then so be it.

I press my thumb down on her lower lip. "Open."

She parts her lips.

My groin hardens. I slide my digit inside her mouth, and she swirls her tongue around it. She bites down on my thumb and my dick lengthens. My belly knots. I tug my thumb from her mouth, lower my zipper. The sound echoes around the empty space.

She swallows, then gazes up at me, her green eyes glowing in the gathering darkness. So hot, so illicit. Apparently, the parts of me I thought I'd hidden away, have been right there, under the surface, waiting to reveal themselves. All they had needed was the right trigger. In this case, her.

Everything I had sacrificed and deprived myself of, everything I'd starved myself of and emptied out, to make space for Him... All of it...had been for nothing. I thought I'd come closer to Him, to perfection, and that had been my failing. For in the very act of aiming to aspire to be like Him, I'd allowed my ego to intrude. I'd dared to think I was anywhere close to Him, and that had been my greatest shortcoming. I am very much a man, with all of the imperfections and weaknesses... It's just that it had all been carefully hidden behind the cloak I had donned. I had allowed myself to be taken in by the image I had presented to the world... I had begun to believe in my own story, the one I'd spun for my flock. So much so, I'd thought I could fool God into believing it too... I should have known better. All this time, I'd been setting myself up for a fall and not realized it...

Until she came along. Oh, how I hate her, how I am grateful to her. How I need to find a way to reward her. But first... I pull out my cock, and pump it once, twice.

Her breathing grows heavy. Her chest heaves. She reaches her hand out, and I click my tongue. "So greedy, so impatient... Oh, my darling, Eve."

"Ava," she whispers. "My name's Ava."

"The enchantress who caused my downfall."

She stiffens, lifts her chin, "Edward... I—"

"Shh," I admonish her, "don't talk."

She purses her lips and nods.

I reach down, dig my fingers into the back of her hair and apply pressure. She moves closer, tips up her chin. I drag the crown of my cock across her lips and she licks up the trail of precum. My balls tighten and my groin hardens.

"Open," I growl, and she parts her lips. I feed my cock to her. Piston my hips forward and the head of my cock bumps up against the back of her throat. She chokes; spit drools from the corners of her mouth, but I don't release her. Something about how she stares up at me with tears dripping from her eyes, turns me on even further. My dick thickens and my thighs spasm. I tug on her hair, yank her head back and a groan bleeds from her.

I push her head forward and my dick disappears inside her mouth.

*Dear God, why is that the single most erotic thing I have ever seen in my life?*

*Will you forgive me for using Your name for when I am the most aroused I have ever been? Not even during the times before I'd become a priest, when I'd experimented with my sexuality, when I'd tried to understand what it was that I had been missing all my life... The searching that had finally led me to You, my Lord... Never, at any of those times, had I felt like this. Is it wrong that I am breaking this vow, right here under Your roof? Can a relationship as close as ours break overnight? If I walk away from You after this, will You ever forgive me? How can I continue doing what I do, knowing I have broken my vow to You? Of everything I've done...this...this feels the most wrong. I'd pledged to keep myself empty, to stay a vessel for Your presence... Yet here I am, turning my back on everything I once held dear. Will You ever forgive me, my Lord, for I cannot stop myself? Will You think less of me, now that I have strayed from Your path?*

I thrust in and out of her mouth, and she lets me. She holds my gaze, allows me to use her, as I increase the pace. In-out-in, my fingers clenched in her hair, as I slap my hand out and smack my palm into the wall next to me. My heart thuds in my chest, my pulse rate ratchets up, lust...heat...adrenaline laces my blood, as I pump in and out of her mouth.

I pull out until I am poised at the edge of her lips, then plunge back in. Her entire body jolts. Her chest heaves, more spit drools from her mouth to wet her dress. She juts out her chin, and the underside of my cock scrapes across her teeth. My thigh muscles coil and a ripple of heat seizes me. The tension curled at the base of my spine tightens, knots, curls in on itself until I can't breathe, can't think. Can't do anything but pull out of her and grip the base of my cock. "Fuck!" I growl aloud. "Fuck. Fuck. Fuck." I lurch back as I squeeze down to stop myself coming.

I tug her head back and she glances up at me.

"Open your mouth," I growl.

She parts her lips, tips her chin –up, and my balls draw up. I pump myself one last time then pull out as I come.

# 17

Ava

The tendons of his throat flex, his brow draws down, he closes his eyes, and a groan rumbles up his massive chest as he comes, shooting white streams of cum across my face. He continues to pump himself, the muscles of his forearms flexing, his biceps tensing as he seems to come and come across my mouth, my cheeks, my hair. I'm decorated in Edward, and hell, if it isn't the most erotic situation I've ever found myself in.

His chest heaves, his shoulders bunch, he lowers his head, opens his eyes and fixes those brilliant brown eyes on me.

My breath catches. *Jesus... No...no...no, I can't be calling to Jesus, not when I am here in His House.* But honestly, there is no better word I can use to encapsulate just how hot this guy is. Edward, I mean. The hot priest who glares down at me like he hates me. His gaze burns into me, like he...feels so much more for me. All the unbidden, unwanted, unseen, unheard carnal desires that I've harbored since I saw Edward on screen... The vampire, I mean, this time. Though Edward, the priest, is far sexier, bigger, taller, more present, more real, more vibrating with pent-up frustration, more ripped, more tatted up, more hurt… There's something hot and hungry and sad inside of him that makes me want to gather his head close to my bosom and cradle him there. A final burst of ropy white cum snakes across my face. I flick out my tongue and lick it up.

He draws in a sharp inhale. Then leans down, scoops up some of the liquid from my cheeks and holds it to my lips. I open my mouth and lock my lips around his digits and lick it clean. He continues to feed me his cum and I eat it from his fingertips like the starving, filthy girl that I am. Then he rubs the remaining fluid into my cheeks. I swallow, squeeze my thighs together. Why is that so hot, so filthy…so incredibly demeaning, but dirty as all hell and so, so sexy?

He drags his thumb across my lower lip, then leans down to nip on it.

I shudder.

He leans back, wraps his fingers around the back of my neck and I shiver. His every action is so intense, so…so dominant, and he's barely done anything to me yet. I'd been right. The moment he'd taken off the persona worn to the world, I'd met a completely different side of him… A part of him that could completely consume me with his intensity.

A pulse tics at his temple, his shoulders bunch, and the planes of his chest seem to ripple with an unseen tension.

How long had it been since he'd last come? Did he allow himself to masturbate? Probably not; not someone as dedicated as Edward. So why had he chosen to break his vow of chastity, and with me?

I open my mouth to ask him, but he shakes his head as he pulls me to my feet. He tips up my chin, leans over me, then presses his lips to mine. He swipes his tongue inside my mouth, tangles his tongue with mine, tilts his head, deepens the kiss, sucks on my tongue until it feels like he's consuming me completely.

Heat flushes my skin, the blood thumps at my temples, my toes curl, and my fingers itch to touch him, but I lock them into fists.

When he finally draws away, both of us are panting. He stares into my eyes, "Forgive me," he mutters, "for what I am going to do to you."

"You can do anything you want."

"That's what I am afraid of."

"I'm not," I retort.

His lips kick up. "How can you be so perfect?" He rakes his gaze across my features. "So gorgeous, so completely flawless?"

"I am not," I protest.

"You are, where it counts, Eve."

"And where is that?"

He places his palm over my left breast. "Your soul, your heart... You have this innate goodness in you, something you were born with, something I have been searching for all my life."

"And you found it..." I glance about the space, "here?"

"And here." He taps the space above my heart. "Your beauty shines through, a mirror to the world, an innocence that declares itself unafraid of anything that comes your way."

"Except you." I swallow. "I am scared, Edward."

"Of what?"

"Of this, what is between us...this which is so new, so wrong, so illicit."

"And it is the most difficult thing I have done in my entire life."

"What?"

"Open myself to you." He lowers his head until his nose bumps mine. "You make me realize that I am not perfect. That I was wrong in thinking I have accomplished so much, when really, I am only getting started."

I take in his gaze, the color on his cheeks, the slight twitch in his left eyebrow. "I... I don't understand."

"You will, in good time." He steps back, tucks himself inside his pants, then bends his knees and sweeps me up in his arms.

I gasp, "Edward... What—?"

"Shh." He strides out of the booth, up the aisle, and retraces his steps from the last journey we'd made just a few hours ago when he'd carried me in from the accident.

"This is getting to be a habit, you carrying me."

"Let me carry your weight, while I can."

I frown. "What do you mean by that?"

"Just that I used you, now let me take care of you."

"How? By doing more of the same, I hope."

He chuckles. "You, Miss Ava—what's your surname?" He frowns. "I can't believe I've never asked you that."

"It's Erikson, and maybe because you were otherwise occupied?"

"There is that, Ms. Erikson." He nods. "When I am with you, nothing else matters. Not your name or mine. We may as well as be two lights headed on a collision course with each other, with nothing able to get between us."

"Ha, you're also a poet?"

"Only when I'm with you."

"And when you're with Him?"

He stiffens, glances down at me. "With whom?" He frowns. "Who are you talking about."

I blink. "I meant the One Above, the One who is in competition for your affections."

"Not after this." His jaw tics. "I'm afraid I've fallen from His good graces."

"Isn't the Lord meant to forgive as well?"

He tilts his head. "But can I forgive myself?"

He stares straight ahead as he stalks out the back door of the church, down the path that leads to his cottage. He reaches the structure, shoulders open the door again, then walks past the living room, into the bedroom. He places me down on the bed.

He straightens and I grab at his sleeve. "Don't go."

"I'll be right back."

"No." I swallow. "No." My heart hammers against my ribcage. My scalp itches and my skin feels too tight for the rest of me. "Edward, please." I tighten my grip on him. "I've only just gotten you; I don't want to lose you."

His forehead furrows. "You'll never lose me, Eve, don't you see? Whatever is here between us is too strong for anything mortal to come between us."

"And what if...it's not mortal? What if it's some force we can't control, what then?" *What the hell am I saying? Where is this irrational fear coming from?* He's only just taken that crucial step toward me. Hell, he broke his vows for me... Something I'm still not sure how I feel about—so why am I clinging to him like a weak, helpless woman? Which I am not... No way.

He places his hand over mine. "I'm only going to get you some water. I promise, I'll be right back."

I nod, release him, watch as he prowls away, long-legged, powerful muscles of his thighs flexing under the fabric of his pants, the muscles of his tight arse coiling and uncoiling with every step he takes. I swallow, sit up in the bed, and pull up my knees so I can rest my chin on them.

He walks out and I turn my attention to the room. Other than the single bed, which I am on, there's a study table and a chair pushed up against the window. A wooden closet in the far corner, it's surface gleaming in the rays of the setting sun that pours through the window. I reach over and click on the lamp next to the bed. Blinking at the illumination, I glance up as he walks back in. He offers me a glass of water, urges me to drink it completely, then places the glass to the side, next to his phone.

He sits down on the bed. "We really do need to talk, now."

# 18

Edward

"About what?" She stares up at me, her face shining from where I'd rubbed my cum into her cheeks.

*My cum.*

*My woman.*

*Mine.*

And Him... What about the One to whom I'd dedicated my entire life? I lean back, putting distance between us. Her gaze sweeps down, before she raises her gaze back toward me. And I know she notices. And I shouldn't be doing this. I shouldn't be acting in such a shitty manner, not after I've come this far. But old habits die hard.

Apparently, there's a part of me, deep inside, that still holds onto the kernel of the man I'd thought I'd once been—unshakeable, focused, emptied of all personal emotions... So, I could receive His grace. His blessings. All that had mattered once was my devotion, my loyalty, my dedication to do what was right.

And what is *right*?

Her?

Me?

This unshakeable connection that I feel to her…the likes of which I'd only felt once before…When I'd been called to Him.

When I'd looked at Him and felt the kind of deep, intense rapport that had warned that it wouldn't get easier. That I'd do anything for Him; that I'd turn my world upside down, tear down any barriers that could come between us; that I'd open up my heart and soul to Him. And I had. And look where that had gotten me.

"I want you." I glare at her flushed features. "I need you, but you have to understand that this isn't easy for me."

"I understand, Edward." She folds her fingers together. "I can't even imagine how difficult this must be for you. When was the last time you slept with anyone?"

"Before I was ordained."

"Which was what—?"

"Five," he mutters, "five years ago."

"And you've never slept with anyone since?" She gulps.

"Not even in my dreams. Not until you came along."

"You've slept with me in your dreams?"

"I have stopped myself from doing everything I know I can…and sleeping isn't one of those things." I allow my lips to curl.

"Right." She shivers, folds her arms even tighter around her knees and I am sure if I touched her between her legs, I'd find her wet and aching and empty and hot and waiting for me. Fuck me. I haven't even touched her properly yet, and the length in my pants insists it's time. That I shouldn't wait any longer. And that's a laugh. All these years, I've never been interested, not once, in anything except my need to please Him, the One Above… And now that I've taken the first step out from under His aegis…it seems my past is coming back to embrace me with a vengeance.

I rise to my feet, glance down to where she has her fingers wrapped around each other. The skin across her knuckles stretches white, and for a second, I want to close the distance between us, to hold her close to me and tell her I won't hurt her. Except, I'd be lying if I said that.

"Are you nervous?"

She nods.

"Good," I square my shoulders, "you should be."

"You're scaring me, Ed."

"That was my intention."

"It is?"

I allow my lips to twist.

"How much have you learned about what happened to us Seven when we were taken?"

"The incident?" she asks, her voice cautious.

"The incident." I say the word without changing my tone. Good. At least, the years of trying to control my feelings have turned out to be of some use.

I rise to my feet and begin to pace. "You are aware that the seven of us were kidnapped and held for close to a month before the cops found us?"

"Is that how you got the scar?"

I stiffen, then turn to glare at her, "Is that what you heard?"

"It's what I guessed." She raises a shoulder. "The women have mentioned the incident, but they never go into it in detail."

"Trust me, it's best that way." I set my jaw. "Suffice to say that what the kidnappers did to each of us..." I fold my fingers into fists at my side. "It changed our lives forever. It changed who we were. Changed our futures, changed how we perceived ourselves. It set us apart from the rest of the boys our age then and ensured that no matter how far we ran or how much we grew up, the specter of what happened to us would never be too far off from our minds."

"Why...why are you telling me this?" She twists her fingers together in front of her.

"I am not sure." I stare down into her face. It's the truth. Maybe I started out because I want her to understand the reasons behind what I am about to do? Maybe I am trying to make excuses for myself? Maybe... I am trying to lessen the coming blow. Maybe... I am just a bastard who is selfish enough to set aside the one good thing that has crossed his path in all these years by hurting her. But it's for her own good. It is. No good will come of this, not when there is no future for either of us. Not when she could do much better than me. My nerve endings jangle and I ignore it. There is someone out there who can give her everything I can't. I am doing this for her own good. I am. I lock my elbows at my sides, take a step back from her.

"This, whatever it is between us, ends here, Ava."

"What?" She blinks. "What are you saying?"

"I can't see you again. You understand that, right?"

"But," she gapes…"I thought now that you'd—"

"Come in your mouth, everything would turn out right?"

She pales. "Why are you doing this?"

"What?'

"Trying to make me hate you?"

*Because it's the only way I can rectify what I've done to you, by ensuring that you hate me enough to never look at me again.*

"Clearly, I am not trying hard enough, if you are still here talking to me." I roll my shoulders.

"You don't fool me." She rises to her feet. "You're doing this because you think it will drive me away from you. You're wrong about it, though."

"Oh?"

"I understand what it means to have found your calling, only to question your beliefs related to it."

"Do you now?"

She nods. "When I told my parents that I wanted to be a dancer, they flipped out. They thought I was joking, that it was a temporary passion, that I'd come to my senses and move beyond it, that it was just a hobby that I was taking too seriously, that I'd outgrow it. They tried everything to stop me from dropping out of university to pursue it."

"Did they succeed?"

"What do you think?" Her lips quirk.

"I think you are perceptive and strong and persistent. That despite your fragile appearance you have a backbone of steel."

She tilts her head, "You've given it some thought, then?"

*I've given you a lot of thought.*

"Once you set your mind on something, you don't give up." My heart begins to thud. I hear my words and I know it's a sign, that she can be stubborn and persistent and focused on what she wants. All the more reason it's important that she not waste her talents on me. "Which is why you'll understand what I am going to say next."

"What?" she whispers. "What is it?"

"I cannot give up my faith for you, Ava."

# 19

Ava

"Nobody's asking you to give up your faith, only your vocation." I tip up my chin. I wish I could be selfless enough to tell him that it doesn't matter, that I don't expect him to turn his back on his life's work, his ideals, his love and devotion for the One Above; but I'm only a woman. A flawed—and now morally corrupt woman, since I'd seduced a priest. OMG, I had, hadn't I? Add that to the list of my sins, as well—along with being selfish enough to want him for myself. Is it right to wish that he'd belong only to me? That he'd turn away from the One who's occupied his life and his thoughts for so long and give all his attention solely to me? Is it right to want to take him away from his flock, his people, the ones he'd, no doubt, helped heal along their life's journeys, as well?

Is it right for me to be this selfish, to want him for myself? Will he allow me to be this self-centered? Does it even matter what I want, when clearly, he's already made up his mind?

"Tell me, Edward," I insist, "why can't you, for once, think only of yourself?"

"Because I can't." He drags his fingers through his hair. "After the incident, I was on a journey of self-destruction. From the age of twelve when I was kidnapped to nearly nineteen, I hung out with the rest of the Seven, and yet in many ways, I wasn't one of them. They liked to get drunk and take part in fights they organized, first on our school grounds, and later, in a deserted parking lot outside London. They were good at it though... Me? I was into a different kind of self-destruction."

He glances at me, then away, and begins to pace.

"What...what kind?" I sit back down on the bed, watch him as he walks to the window, glances out, then grips the edge of the windowsill. "Drugs, sex, getting into fights where none of the Seven were around to back me up," his voice tapers off.

"So, you were trying to hurt yourself?"

He turns to glance at me over his shoulder. "I did a damn good job of it, too. By rights, I should have ended up dead, or worse," he grimaces, "if it weren't for Baron."

"Baron?" I scowl. "The missing one of the Seven?"

"Oh, he isn't missing. He chooses to stay away."

"Why is that?"

"It's the only way he could cope with what had become of him, of us, I suppose." He raises his shoulders. "Who knows what went on in that mind of his? If the rest of us were trying to hurt ourselves, Baron took it a step further."

"What do you mean?"

"While I was dabbling with ways to cause myself pain so I could forget what had happened to me, Baron was... Let's just say, his appetite for self-destruction was more vicious than mine."

"How's that?"

He turns to face me. "He took risks with his life. Not only was he a brilliant hacker, but he was also into extreme sports. He loved adventure sports, training for the kinds of expeditions from which coming back alive is not certain. He kept pushing himself, challenging himself at every turn, and that was only the tip of what he told us."

"And you know this, how?"

"While I was imploding inside, Baron was challenging himself, pushing himself to see how far he could go before he could die, if that makes sense." He widens his stance. "In some ways, it made him the most clear-headed of all of us Seven. Which is why he's the one who found me one night in a drug den, shot out of my skull, OD'd, and perhaps a breath away from dying."

"So, he found you and saved you that day?"

"That's one way of putting it." He chuckles. "He gave me holy hell when I regained consciousness in the hospital. It's Baron who checked me into a retreat. A very expensive sober living place, paid for by my family's money, of course."

"Of course," I say dryly. What little I know about the Seven points to the behavior that they make sure they always get their money's worth out of deals. Still, it was fair, I suppose. Baron came to his friend's' rescue and took the very important step of having him checked into a treatment facility. Then, in a strike of poetic justice, he made sure Edward paid for it out of his own pocket. Well, why not? It's one way of ensuring he felt the consequences of his actions, right?

"Like I said, I owe my life to him."

"And you're telling this to me, why?"

He raises his chin and fixes me with that stern glare that has my panties going damp at once. Hell, why is it that he can turn me on by just looking at me?

One side of his lips twists as if he's aware of exactly what I'm thinking, then he rotates his shoulders and cracks his neck. The sound shudders across the space, sinks into my blood, coils down into the space between my legs, which is already empty and wet and throbbing and— I turn away from him. "What is it you are trying to say, Ed?" I ask again.

"That when I was at my lowest, in the drug-filled haze, and fighting between life and death in the hospital, I had a vision."

"The proverbial light at the end of the long tunnel?" I say, only half-joking.

"Yes," he replies, all amusement wiped from his face. "I know I was dead when he found me. I know I stayed in that dead space for an hour before they revived me at the hospital. When I opened my eyes, I knew what I had to do."

"To become a priest," I say dully.

He nods. "Whatever I felt in that time... And it felt like I had journeyed to the depths of time. I felt like I had been gone much longer, you know... And it wasn't anything I saw or felt or heard... It was just a realization that I woke up with. A sense of peace, of contentment, even; something I'd never felt in the years since the incident, maybe even earlier. It was that complete rightness of it that led me to joining the seminary."

"So, you felt a divine calling and you made your choice?"

"You're not listening," he snaps. "It was not a choice. It was an awareness. I woke up one day and it was simply there, and I never questioned it."

"Not even now?" I take a step toward him. "When this—realization between us too is just there. It's not what you or I asked for. It's simply a connection, a state of being, something I don't even question —" He raises his hand, but I continue, "And neither do you. I know it; don't deny it."

"It is there," He narrows his gaze on me. "I can't deny it. But I also cannot embrace it."

"No, no, no." I shake my head. My heart begins to thud. A hole opens up in my stomach, grows bigger, begins to swallow me. This can't be happening, it can't. "No." I hear myself say the word aloud as if trying to deny what I sense is coming. What I know he's going to do and which I hate with every fiber in my body, and yet, I am powerless to stop, damn him.

"Listen to me." He takes a step forward and I skitter back.

"Don't say it, don't," I beg him. "Don't do it."

"I have to."

"Please, give us a chance."

"You don't know what you are asking."

"Oh, believe me, I do." I dig my heels into the floor, lock my fingers together, "I know exactly what I am asking of you, and if you deny it, I know it's going to make you hate yourself for life."

"Not more than I already do." His lips twist. "I am so sorry, Ava, but this is how it has to be."

"It doesn't. You can change it. You have the power to do it."

"The only one with the power is Him." He jerks his chin upward. "I am but His servant, His to command."

"I am yours to command," I choke out the words. "Doesn't that mean anything to you?"

He winces. "It does. It means far too much, and that's the problem." He peers into my face, "Don't you see that?"

"The only thing I see is a coward who can't face the truth, who can't see what's right there in front of him, who refuses to acknowledge the reality of his situation."

"Which is?"

"That you don't belong to Him anymore. You may deny it all you want, but you're mine now Edward, and nothing can change that."

"Except me." He draws himself up to his full height. "I deny it, I deny you. I don't want you. I choose Him over you."

"No." I shake my head.

"Yes." He says it with a tone of finality. "Yes."

"Don't do it."

"It's done." He folds his arms across his chest.

"This is it then?"

"It would seem that way."

My chin wobbles, my hands and legs shake, and a hot sensation stabs at my chest. My knees tremble and I fold my fingers at my sides. "So, this is goodbye?"

His features shutter and his lips firm. He watches me with that detached expression on his face that I hate so much. The one which indicates that I have already lost him. So why am I still standing here?

Turning, I head for the door.

"Ava"

My heart stutters and hope blooms in my chest.

I turn to find him holding out my handbag, "Don't forget this."

I swallow down the emotion that surges up my throat, march toward him, snatch up my bag. "I hate the day I set eyes on you. I hate that He brought you into my life" I say in a low tone. "One day...one day you are going to realize that the choice you made here was all wrong, but by then, it's going to be too late."

Turning, I walk out.

# 20

Edward

She's gone. She left me. I had allowed her to walk out of here. I had encouraged her to walk out of here.

I didn't stop her. Didn't ask her to come back. Didn't run after her and grab her and haul her back to me. I'd watched as she'd stepped out of my home, and the door had snicked shut behind her.

Then, I had glanced around the familiar surroundings of the place that had once brought me so much comfort—the serenity, the sparseness, the starkness of it, a reminder that I had made my choice. I had chosen the greater good over my selfish needs. I had chosen my loyalty, my devotion, my faith. I had chosen Him. After one brief slip up when I had come so close to realizing how it could have been between us, I had walked away. I had reached inside myself, drawn on the last reserves of my self-possession, and I had turned away from her. I had held onto my principles, *everything that I hold dear...*

So why is there a nagging pain under my rib cage? Why is my stomach knotted and twisted? Why are my shoulder muscles bunched up? Why is there a heaving sensation in my guts? The bile bubbles up my throat and my belly churns. I pivot, race to the bathroom, and lean over the commode. I empty out all the contents of my stomach, and dry heave until I can't hold myself upright anymore. Managing to flush away the disgusting mess, I rise to my feet, head for the sink and rinse out my mouth, before sinking to the floor.

*Fuck, fuck, fuck.*

I'd slipped up and come all over her face and it had felt like I had marked her, branded her, tied her to me irrevocably. Just like He had staked his claim on me.

Then I had found my conscience and turned my back on her—and the anguish in her eyes, the hate and helplessness in her features, combined with her vulnerability, had me reaching for her again. Only I hadn't. I had told her that I denied that she was mine. I had lied.

She is mine.

Nothing changes that.

Just as I belong to Him.

And He comes first.

He always has.

Nothing can change that.

Nothing. Not even her. Right?

*Everything that I hold dear...*

My stomach churns again, my insides twist, and I turn to the commode just in time to dry heave again and again. By the time I sink back to the floor, I am shattered. It feels like I have puked my very guts out... And my heart... And my soul. Everything of meaning to me has deserted me.

Except Him. I still have Him. I lurch up to my feet, splash cold water on my face at the sink. I dry my face, then turn and walk over to the cross hanging on the wall in my bedroom. I sink to my knees next to the bed...next to where I'd lowered her recently. I turn away from it, tip my chin up toward the skies. I raise my arms, close my eyes.

*Forgive me, Lord, for I have sinned.*

*I couldn't control myself.*

*I allowed myself to be weak.*

*How should I punish myself this time, my Lord?*
*How many times should I atone for what I have done wrong?*

I empty my mind of all thoughts and wait. And wait. Sink inside, into the deep, quiet space inside of me where no one else is allowed... Where there's an infinite expanse, waiting to be filled by Him. His voice. His presence. I wait and wait. And the answer seeps into my subconscious mind.

*Twenty.*

I wince. Almost ask Him if he is sure, but of course, He is. And I am not one to question the Lord. I rise to my feet, walk over to my closet and pull out my discipline. I peel off my shirt, walk over to the center of the room, then whip myself. Pain pulses up my spine, my skin gives, blood seeps down my back. The pent-up pressure inside me lessens and my muscles loosen. I whip myself again and again. By the time I reach ten, my arms ache and my back hurts. Blood runs down to drip onto the floor. I draw in a breath, whip myself again, and the strands of the whip curl around me, to slice open the skin on my belly. I grunt, allow the pain to absolve me, whip myself faster and faster. Sweat pools under my armpits, drenches my back and sinks into my blood. Pain thuds at my nerve-endings, at my temples, behind my eyes. I don't stop until I hit twenty, then lower the discipline to my side. I glance up at the wooden cross on the wall, my limbs trembling, my throat dry.

*Do You forgive me now my Lord? Am I still Yours?*

I squeeze my eyes and wait, wait.

There's no answer.

# 21

Edward

"What are you punishing yourself for?"

I drag my attention away from the window of Sinclair's conference room. The very same place where, not long ago, the six of us had stood, discussing the disbursement of funds for the new non-profit that Sinclair had suggested. The same one that I am hoping we can put to good use in initiatives I consider worthy.

"What do you mean, punishing?" I turn to face Sinclair, who's sprawled out in his chair. He seems, for all the world, like a man at peace with his world, which, of course, he is.

He's married and Summer, his wife, only recently discovered she's pregnant. Between him and Saint and Damian—that's already three anticipated arrivals in our circle. Given how madly in love they are, I wouldn't be surprised if the rest of them follow suit shortly. They deserve it, all of them. Every single slice of happiness that comes their way. After everything we've been through, it's only fair that the rest of them have the best years of their lives to look forward to.

*And you? What about you?*

I am on a different path. Like Baron. Even before the incident, the two of us had always been different from the rest of the Seven. And then the incident, while it had brought us together... In some ways, it had also highlighted how disparate we were from the rest.

"I mean," Sinclair leans forward, "you look like shit, Father."

No kidding. I rub my unshaven jaw. It's been two days since I saw her. Two days since I shaved. Two days since I atoned, or tried to compensate, for my slip up. The Lord hasn't spoken to me since.

Not that I am worried. I've gone for days...months in the past, when He'd retreated to the Light. He'll return to me... He has to... He always does. He's done so on the other occasions when I had erred. None of them had been as serious as this, though.

I'd chosen Him though, hadn't I? I had turned my back on the one good thing that had come across my path. I had torn out my heart and willingly offered it to the Lord. *So, what more does He want from me?*

I clear my throat, then turn to stare out the window. "Why did you want to talk to me?"

"Baron."

I still, then compose my features into one of nonchalance before I turn to him. "You heard from him?"

"That's what I was going to ask you." He scowls at me. "You were the one who heard from him last, isn't that right?"

I nod. "Nothing since that last letter.

"Hmm." Sinclair leans his elbows on the table, then presses his fingers together.

"Doesn't it strike you as odd that he'd write, out of the blue, to warn us of the Mafia?'

"It's Baron." I raise my shoulders. "Who knows what prompts him to do what he does?"

"I thought you guys were close."

"Close?" I laugh. "That's not how I would put it." I drag my fingers through my hair. "More like, at loggerheads."

"Enough to keep sniping at each other all the time. Enough that when you were at your lowest, he tracked you down and hauled your arse out of that drug-den you'd crawled into."

I set my jaw.

Sinclair folds his arms across chest, "You thought you and Baron came out of the incident the worst, so it gave the two of you some kind of permission to form your own pity club within the Seven—"

"Pity club?" I scowl.

"You forget we swore to always have each other's backs, no matter what. And that included giving the two of you space when needed."

"The lot of you gave us space?" I laugh. "None of you had an inkling of what we went through—"

"Only because you never shared," Sinclair snaps. "Do you realize how frustrating it is that the rest of us have been open about what happened to us? While you and Baron..." His jaw firms, "The two of you clammed up, as if there was some secret that bound the two of you, something that you didn't dare talk about, in case—"

"In case—?" I tilt my head.

"In case, talking about it would force you to acknowledge what actually happened."

"And is that so bad?"

"It is." He rises to his feet and grips the edge of the table. "If you want to heal, then you need to open up, Father. If not to one of us, then to her."

"Who?"

"Cut the bullshit, Ed. We know."

"Know?"

He nods.

"Know what?"

"That you and that delectable dancer of yours have a thing going on," a new voice answers from the doorway that connects the conference room to Sinclair's office.

I glance toward the man who fills the doorway, then groan, "Oh, no."

"Oh, yes." Weston walks in... Or rather, is dragged in by a very excited Max, who prances around on a leash. Weston unhooks his leash, and Max dashes toward Sinclair, who bends down to pet him.

"Hey, little bugger," he croons, "you missed me, did you?" Max barks, licks Sinclair's face, places his paws on his £7000 suit. Sinclair doesn't flinch. He scratches behind the dog's ears and Max positively whimpers in ecstasy, before dropping his paws back on the floor. The dog races around the table toward me. I hold my hand in front of his nose, then mirror Sinclair's gesture by digging my fingers behind Max's ears. The dog huffs, tongue lolling, before pulling away and racing around back to Sinclair, who once more pets him.

"Good practice for when the little one comes along, eh?" Weston walks over to deposit the leash on Sinclair's table. "My, how you've unbent since the snarling, growling man you used to be, not long ago."

"Speak for yourself." Sinclair straightens, and Max settles at his feet. "I still have my edge."

"Wait until the patter of little feet sounds on your office floor. Then we'll see," Weston retorts.

"Office floor?" He glances around, "Why would I bring the kid in here?"

"You mean Summer hasn't told you?"

"What?"

"That she plans to split parenting duties half in half with you."

"As she should." Sinclair scowls. "Still, doesn't mean I'd bring the kid to office."

"You would if you had a creche in the office." Saint prowls in. "I am all for it, given Victoria is only five months from giving birth and I, for one, wouldn't want to be parted from the kid for that long—"

"So, you are going to bring the kid to work?" I ask.

"Probably not." Saint smirks.

"Then?" I frown.

"Ideally, I'd work from home. Hell, I could work from anywhere, and this way, I can spend time with my family. Best of both worlds."

"Of course." The three of us turn to Sinclair who stares between us. "What?"

"You going to shift to a home office, as well?"

"I haven't considered it," he rubs the back of his neck, "but it's a possibility. I'll need to discuss it with Summer."

The three of us look at each other, then I chuckle, "It's heartwarming; it really is." I glance around at their faces. "You guys gladden my soul."

"What?" Saint scowls.

"Truly," I jerk my chin at Weston, "it's incredible."

"Care to explain yourself, Father?" Saint drawls.

"Whoever said the Lord works in mysterious ways surely knew what they were talking about."

Sinclair arches an eyebrow. "If you think speaking in riddles will pique our attention?" He knocks his knuckles against the table. "Then you're right. Out with it, Father."

"All of you assholes brought to heel by the love of a good woman." I raise my gaze heavenward, "Thank you, Lord."

There's silence in the room, then Sinclair chuckles. "Well played, Father. You'd like us to believe that you are the last man standing, but as we all know, that's not true."

"What's not true?" Damian ambles in, his hair streaming about his shoulders. In jeans and sweatshirt, he's the most casually dressed among us. Of course, if Baron were here, he'd probably give Damian a run for his money.

I push the thought from my head, turn to Damian. "Nothing," I say at the same time as Sinclair declares, "That Edward is the last bachelor of the Seven."

"Technically, he isn't, considering we don't know if Baron is married or not." Arpad strolls into the conference room, then shuts the door behind him.

Baron again. Why is there no getting away from the mention of his name right now? Why is he on my mind so much?

Saint barks out a laugh. "Baron? Married? Not likely."

"Hello pot, meet kettle?" I tilt my head at him. "You, Saint, would have been the last man I'd have pegged to get married, and yet—"

"It's you who claims to be still standing strong, when we all know your heart is taken."

"By the One Above," I declare.

"Not that I am refuting that," Sinclair retorts, "but you are a man, after all. So, what if you decided to turn your back on everyday life and chose to become a priest? Underneath that calm demeanor is a man who, perhaps, feels more than any of us. The day you acknowledge it, the day you forgive yourself for what you've been through and stop punishing yourself for what you couldn't change, is the day you realize that you don't have to hide behind the persona of the calm man of the cloth."

I blink at him. "And here I thought I was the preacher."

"Can't preach to the converted, Father." Sinclair's lips twist. "You know everything I am talking about, but the day you acknowledge it is when things will begin to shift for you."

"You think I'm hiding from the world?" I scowl at him.

He meets my gaze with his unblinking one. I glance around the room, take in the expressions on the faces of all my friends. "Wow." I fold my arms across my chest, "Apparently, all of you think I am using my vocation as a crutch."

"Not a crutch..." Weston drums his fingers on his chest. "More like, you were taking your time to process your grief."

"You were the most stubborn of us, Ed. You needed to get your own way when we were boys." Damian widens his stance. "You were also the angriest."

"Angry? Me?" I laugh, "Are you sure you're talking about me."

"Remember the time we came across the boys bullying one of the smaller kids in school? Who's the one who jumped to his rescue?" Arpad asks.

"We all did," I mumble.

"Yes," Arpad nods, "but who started it?"

I stare at him.

"You did," Weston chimes in. "You always took the side of the underdog."

"You had this sense of fair play inside you, which came to the fore when you saw any kind of injustice being done," Saint interjects.

"You were idealistic, the only one of us who wanted to make the world a better place. Yes, you were the angriest amongst all of us, but your triggers were more nuanced." Sinclair places the tips of his fingers together, "You saved your anger for when it would have the best impact."

"Or the worst outcome. As I recall, we were outnumbered that day."

"Ten to seven." Sinclair grins. "Still, we managed to hold our own."

"The fuckers didn't get off easy."

"No," I chuckle, "we managed to whip their asses, all right."

"Though I couldn't complain when the teachers finally separated us." Weston winces.

"And marched us all to the principal's office." Damian smirks.

"Suspended for a week." Saint picks up the narrative.

"And came back to a hero's welcome from the girls." Sinclair's grin widens.

"Couldn't have asked for a better conclusion to that episode," I agree.

"And what about the latest episode, Father?" Sinclair holds my gaze, "What kind of conclusion are you hoping for it?"

"It's concluded," I assert.

"What do you mean?" Sinclair frowns.

"It means," I fold my arms across my chest, "there is nothing to it. I am a priest, or have you forgotten that?"

"Have you ever let us forget it?" Sinclair asks wryly.

"You going passive-aggressive on me, Sinner?" I narrow my gaze on him. "You have something to say, why don't you come out and say it?"

"All I'm saying is, you have used the priesthood to hide from what's important."

"Or maybe I used it to face my fears."

"Did you?" He leans forward with his palms flat on the table. "Is that what you have been doing the last few years?"

I blow out a breath. "Yes. I have been using the discipline that comes with the life of a priest to manage my anger. To channel my frustrations, my hate, my resentment at what happened into something to benefit the greater good of the world."

"Wow," Saint blinks, "you truly do believe you can make a difference to the world?"

"Something like that," I mutter. "Look, it's no big deal. Apparently, the only way I could get past the incident was by dedicating myself to a bigger cause."

"Not that I doubt your cause for one second," Sinclair narrows his gaze on me, "but have you ever thought that maybe looking outside and helping the world was easier than searching inside for the answers?"

I stare at him. "And here I thought you were a shallow, obnoxious, a-hole of the first order with a superiority complex to end all superiority complexes."

Color smears Sinner's cheeks. "That too," he grumbles. "Don't deflect, Father. We are talking about you, not me."

"Yeah, don't turn the attention away from yourself," Damian chimes in.

"We ain't lettin' you go without answering this time," Weston drawls.

I rub the back of my neck, shuffle my feet. "Can't believe I allowed myself to be caught in this situation."

"Nothing you haven't done for the lot of us before." Saint smirks.

"Bet you enjoyed the counsel you gave all of us when we faced crises of confidence in ourselves."

"None of you faced a crisis of faith though," I say it in a low voice, but of course, all of them catch it.

Sinclair sets his jaw, Saint and Weston stiffen, Damian scrutinizes my features, and Arpad? He draws in a breath. "This one's a tough one for you, eh, Father?" he asks softly. "I can only imagine what you are going through right now."

"Can you?" I say bitterly. "When you all met your women, all you had to figure out was how to stop fighting yourselves. How to conquer your ego long enough to come to grips with your feelings for them. You didn't have to fight against your instincts, the very way of life you had carved for yourself, or how to turn your back on the vows which mean more to you than your life."

"Do they Father?" Sinclair asks quietly. "Do they mean more to you than the very breath you take?"

"Yes." I thrust out my chin. "Yes, they do."

"Well, then," he lowers himself back in his chair, "this should be easy, huh?"

# 22

## Edward

When he'd asked the question, I'd agreed at once, yet I can't get his words out of my head. Do my vows mean more than my very breath? Yes, they do. But so does she. It's why I had turned her away. It's why I am here, kneeling in front of the altar in church late at night after the entire world has gone to sleep. I hadn't even bothered going to bed. Instead, I'd stayed up, working on the paperwork needed to ensure that the funding for the various charities I support through FOK media remains uninterrupted. There are always new requests coming in and it is up to me to scan and decide which ones to support next. Children, the elderly, abused women, the most vulnerable among us, including pets... I want all of them to benefit from the dividends of the investments that the Seven have made. While I don't broker any of the deals, the rest of the Seven involve me in all decisions. It's why I am up-to-date with everything and have enough knowledge, if needed, to run the deals myself. Not that I am tempted...I haven't even thought about how it would be to drive those deals until...now... Until her... Until something inside me had wondered how it would be to come home to her every night, to live a normal life with her, to have children like the rest of the Seven are going to do.

I'd thought through all possibilities before enrolling in the seminary. At least, I thought I had. At nineteen, it had been easy to embrace the idea of never falling in love, of never having children. But with everything that has happened so far, I can't help but thinking, what if we were meant to be?

*What if that's why God brought her to me? What if His intention all along was not to test me, but to encourage me to return to the real world?* I blow out a breath.

Clearly, I am spending too much time with the Seven. Their thinking is beginning to rub off on me. It's the only reason I am beginning to question myself so much. I love the Seven like my blood brothers, but when it comes down to it, not one of them has any idea what it's like to be in my shoes. And the only one who does... He is gone. Except for sporadic, snail mail letters once every year or so. Mostly, ones addressed to all of the Seven, assuring us he is alive. Which is why the last one was strange. It had been addressed only to me—I hadn't mentioned that to the Seven. How could I when I, myself, couldn't fathom why he'd done that? Did he mean that the Mafia's threat was centered on me? Why would it be? What do I have that they want? Why would they zero in on me?

Why did they single out me and Baron for what they did when they took us? Maybe I could put that down to being in the wrong place at the wrong time... Maybe. So, what did it mean that Baron had addressed the letter to me?

*And why did you have her cross paths with me, my Lord?*

I close my eyes, raise my head up to the skies, open my arms to His grace. His benevolence. The only reason that I am here today. *Believing in You, throwing myself at Your mercy and asking You for Your forgiveness is what I believe in. It's why I exist today, my Lord, for You saved my soul. You took me in, redeemed me, saved me and gave me purpose. Show me the way now, my Lord. Tell me what to do. Take everything I am—my heart my soul, my life. Take anything you want from me, my Lord, but spare her. Let no*

*harm come to her. Grant unto her, her heart's desires, keep her happy, for that is
all I need. Tell me, my Lord, that you hear me?*

I draw in a breath, and the complex notes of the incense fill my
lungs. The notes of Frankincense and tea-tree tease my nostrils. I
inhale and let the scent waft over me, sink into me, fill my blood and
go to my head. My breath grows deeper and my muscles relax as I
allow my mind to focus on His benevolence, His grace, the complete
self-assuredness with which He's guided me thus far.

*Surely, you'll not let go of me, when I need You the most? When everything
in me insists that the right thing to do is to turn to You.*

And yet my heart... My heart disagrees. My heart persists in
choosing her. *And I can't bear it, my Lord. I can't fail you. I need to find a
way out. I need to return things to what they were. I need You to show me the
way. Tell me what to do, my Lord.*

I pray and pray, but the Lord remains silent. I beg Him, plead
with Him, cajole Him to, at least, talk to me again. But He stays silent.

I stay there until the chill invades my clothes, my skin, until my
knees threaten to give way, and my arms ache from being held aloft.
My thigh muscles tremble, my biceps protest and yet, He remains
silent.

I will not move until You answer me, not this time. I need You to
steer me. Give me a way out. Please. I swallow down the anger, the
hurt, the helplessness that fills my chest and clogs my throat.

Talk to me. You can't be silent, not anymore.

"Father," a voice says from behind me, "can I pray with you?"

I open my eyes, turn to find a man walking up the aisle. As he
draws closer, the acrid scent of cigarette smoke deepens. I take in his
features. He seems familiar. Where have I seen him? Where... He
steps into the beam of light from the illumination above and that's
when it clicks. He's the homeless man I'd seen near the hotel when I'd
gone to see Ava.

"The church is closed, though you are still welcome." I frown,
"How did you get in?"

"I used the side entrance." He nods to the heavy door that leads to
the rectory. Huh. Had I left the door unlocked? But then, I haven't

been thinking clearly since I returned from meeting the rest of the Seven, so I guess I might have forgotten.

The man stops next to me. He glances up at the figure on the cross. "Do you ever wonder if He was happy?"

"You mean Jesus?"

He nods.

"We have no reason to believe otherwise."

"And you, Father?" He turns to me. "Do I have reason to believe otherwise with you?"

I peer down into his features. The uncombed hair falling about his face, his worn-out but clean shirt, the faded jeans that hang off his hips, hinting that he may have been healthier at one point in time, which is, honestly, not too difficult to imagine, and it's not because of his clothes. It's the defeated slump to his shoulders, the faded look in his eyes, as if he's lost all hope. Something I am used to... For it is when they're at their lowest that people most often approach me. Is that why I chose this profession? Because I recognize kindred spirits?

Because I want to cling to that part of me that feeds on my grief, my helplessness, my lack of control I had in that time when I was taken and made to do things which I've never confessed to another. *Maybe to her? Only to her. Where did that thought come from?* I let go of her, remember? I walked away from her. I chose Him. Which is why I am here, ready and willing to do His bidding. To help others. Like this man.

"I am happy with my lot." I hold his gaze. "How can I help you, my child?"

"I need to confess."

# 23

## Edward

"Forgive me Father for I have sinned. It has been…many years since I last confessed."

He swallows, shuffles his feet. The air in the booth grows denser. I shift around to make myself more comfortable. Not that I begrudge the fact that he came this late… But the fact that he interrupted my time, when I was talking to God? I'm not too happy about that. Still, I'd never turn away someone who walks in and asks for help. I lean forward, press the tips of my fingers together, "Go on, son, what would you like to tell me today?"

He fidgets around some more, then leans in, "I… I did something very bad, Father." He pauses, gulps audibly, then blows out a breath. "It was because of me that many lives were spoiled."

"How is that?"

"I helped some bad men when I was much younger. I didn't realize what I was doing then, but it was because of me that many other boys found their futures changed completely." His voice wavers, and he buries his face in his hands. "If I could only turn back time, I'd never have given information of the movements of my classmates to those men."

"How old were you when this happened?"

"I was twelve." His voice breaks. He clears his throat. "I may have put those boys in jeopardy, but it might as well have been me who was taken, as well."

The hair on the nape of my neck rises. "Taken?" I keep all inflection out of my tone. "Who was taken?"

"The boys I spied on." His tone lowers, "I... I couldn't help it, Father. My parents were well-off, but then they lost all their money in a stock market crash. It was only because they'd been patrons who had made large donations that I'd been able to continue my studies in the same school." He shuffles around some more. "And I needed the money." He glances away, then back at me, "I uh, you...you understand what I am trying to say?"

"What did you need the money for?" I can hazard a guess, but I want him to spell it out for me.

"Alcohol... drugs." I sense him shrug.

"You were an addict?"

"That's putting it lightly." He barks out a self-deprecating laugh. "Vodka for breakfast, coke, and not the drinking kind, for lunch, all combined with downers for supper. I was in terrible shape."

I stare through the pattern in the partition, try to make out the expression on his face, but of course, I can't. Who the hell is this guy? Why did he walk in here, of all the churches, and what is he trying to tell me? "How did your school authorities miss that you were an addict?"

"Oh, I was very well-behaved in class, the epitome of the model student. No one, not even my schoolmates, guessed just how far gone I was. If it hadn't been for the fact that my parents lost their fortune..." I sense him shrug, "I could have maintained the status-quo. But it was not to be... I... I—"

"You needed money?"

"You can say that again. And as with all things, when you are desperate, the vultures find you." He drags in a breath. "I was only twelve, Father. You need to understand, I didn't have a clue about the seriousness of what I was going to do."

I curl my fingers into fists, force myself to breathe, breathe. "What did you do?" I finally ask.

"This stranger approached me when I was trying to track down my favorite dealer, who had refused to take my calls because, of course, they know when you are desperate. When you need them the most, that's when they desert you. Have you found that, Father?"

He's blathering now, trying to stray off track, trying to lead himself and me away from the topic at hand. Typical. I've found this pattern to be true of many who come to confession. It's almost like they are in the therapist's chair here. Though, unlike the reasons that lead them to see a therapist, they come here because their conscience doesn't permit them to stay quiet anymore.

Yet, even this far into the narrative, self-preservation kicks in and they try their best to wriggle out of it, to place the blame elsewhere.

"This stranger," I prompt him. "What did he want from you?"

"When I finally tracked down my dealer, he was waiting for me."

"Who?" I query. "The dealer?"

"The man," he snaps. "Are you following me, Father?"

I twist my lips. "I am right there with you."

"He was well-dressed, in an expensive suit, sunglasses, a hat... Looked like something out of a Mafia film."

My heart begins to thud. Sweat beads my temple. "Is that what he was? The Mafia?"

"So, I found out later." He swallows. "He wanted me to get information on some boys."

My pulse thuds at my temples. "What kind of information?"

"About their daily routines. How they got to school every day, where they went to football practice, what else they did in the after-school hours."

"So, you did it?"

"Yeah." I sense him nod. "I got him all the information he wanted."

"And he rewarded you?"

"For my sins?" he says quietly. "Asshole, gave me drugs and kept doing so for the next... I don't know, many years. They made me dependent on them. I ended up being reliant on them for my next fix, something they exploited, in every way possible."

"And do you still work for them?" I keep my voice even.

"What do you think?" He laughs bitterly, "Once you've interacted with them, they never let you go."

I rub at the pain that stabs at my chest. What the hell am I doing, encouraging him to speak? I should ask him to shut up. I should get the hell out of here, before I do something I'll regret. I lock my fingers together, tuck my elbows into my sides.

"And the boys on whom you reported. What about them?"

He stays silent.

"You've come this far. Get it all off your chest. Pour out all the worries inside of you to make space for the Holy Spirit." I narrow my gaze on the screen and what I can see of his profile. *Go on, you asshole, confirm to me what I already know. Do it already. Give me the chance to get even for everything that happened to me and my friends. Say it. Do it.*

"The b-boys," he stutters, "the...they were kidnapped."

My heart stops, then picks up speed and slams into my chest. The blood thuds at my temples. My palms grow clammy and I flex my fingers.

"What school?" I force myself to say the words, "Which school did these boys attend?"

He draws in another breath, seems to hesitate.

"Get out everything, my son," I prompt him. "Every last memory associated with what happened. Lay it all out, so you can make a fresh start.

He swallows, moves around again, then finally lets out a sigh. "St. Lucian's," he mumbles.

I freeze. "St. Lucian's?"

So, he definitely is talking about me and rest of the Seven. Not that there had been any doubt in my mind. Too much of what he'd told me matched what had happened to us. But I had to be completely sure.

"Only the most exclusive private school in the country," he scoffs. "You wouldn't think kids from such an exclusive school would be involved in something like that, would you?"

I stare at his profile through the screen. This is the person responsible for turning the lives of me and my friend's upside down. If he hadn't shared information on us... Someone else would have? Maybe. Maybe not. Right now, as the facts stand, it is this man—this pathetic, wretched excuse of a human being—who shared information on us, who is partially responsible for the emotionally deficient, heartless men that we have become. And maybe he hasn't fared that well either. But it doesn't change the fact that if he hadn't reported on us, if he had turned down the offer of the Mafia, there's a small chance we might have turned out normal. Normal? Hah! What's that? What do I know about it? Except, that it is what most of the Seven now have.

Not me, though.

Never me.

And this guy... This bastard sitting on the opposite side of the screen is responsible for the sodden, tragic-comedy farce that my life has become. My vision tunnels and my senses pop. I rise to my feet, walk around and yank the curtain open.

The man stares up at me. "Father?" He frowns. "Is something wrong?"

"Nothing." I smile at him. "Everything is just how it should be. You couldn't have picked a better church and a more apt priest to confess your sins to."

His shoulders sag in relief. "Thank you, Father. I'm so grateful that you listened and did not judge."

"Me, judge?" I chuckle. "No, I wouldn't do that. Why would I? After all, kids are young and resilient. They bounce back from such traumatic memories, don't they? Assuming they survived to tell the tale, that is?"

"Oh, they did." He bobs his head up and down. "They all survived, thank God for that."

"You sure 'bout that?"

"What?"

"That it was better that they survived?" I lean down and peer into his face, "Are you positive it was better that they survived?"

He blinks rapidly. "Uh... Yes. Of course. I mean, better to live than to die, right?"

"Wrong."

He gapes at me. "F...father, is everything all right? You...you... seem pale."

"Do I?" I reach out and clamp my fingers around his neck. "Wonder why that is?"

His gaze widens. I tighten my grasp and he coughs, then grabs at my hand. I haul him up to his feet.

"Wh... what are you doing?" he chokes out.

"What does it look like?"

I drag him out of the booth and toward the altar.

"Father..." He tries to speak, but I squeeze his neck, apply even more pressure. His body jerks. He opens and shuts his mouth, then digs his fingernails into my wrist. Pain shivers up my arm; all noise in my head fades.

"Do you know who I am?" I stare into his widened gaze. "Answer me."

He opens and shuts his mouth, but no words emerge.

"Nod, if you recognize me," I order.

"I... I..." He gags. "Edward Chase." He finally says, " I know who you are."

I blink. "And yet you came to me to confess?" I say in a low voice. "Why is that?"

His gaze widens, but he doesn't speak.

"Tell me, what game are you trying to play with me? Why did you walk into my church? Why choose to confess to me?" I squeeze harder, and his eyes bulge. He begins to choke, to scratch at my wrists. His shoulders shudder, tears leak out from the corners of his eyes.

"Did you think you'd get Absolution for your sins? After all isn't Absolution an integral part of the Sacrament of Penance, is that why you came to me? To be forgiven? And who better to do so than one of the Seven who was a victim of your wrong doing?"

He shakes his head, and a cold sensation grips my chest. My belly knots, and my pulse rate slows down.

"Or maybe you came, knowing if you confessed to me, it would push me over the edge. Maybe you hoped I'd lose control enough to grant you eternal redemption. After all, it's thanks to what you did that I found my faith. So, it's only right that I use the authority conferred on me to grant you eternal peace."

His gaze widens.

"Normally I take the vow of confidentiality during confession very seriously, but in your case, I'll be making an exception."

He tries to speak, but only a choking sound emerges.

"By the power vested in me my by the Church, I absolve you of your sins, in the name of the Father, the Son and the Holy Ghost." My vision tunnels. Anger thrums at my temples. I release the grip on his throat with one hand while I continue to choke him with other. I raise my right hand. "In the name of the Father." I squeeze his throat, as I lower my hand. "Son." I increase the pressure on his throat as I swipe my free hand to my left, "Holy Spirit." I bear down with every last sliver of strength left in me. "Amen." I complete the benediction by moving my hand to my right.

When I loosen my grip on him, he slumps down to the floor. I lower my arms to my sides, then glance up at the figure on the cross above me. "So, this is what you wanted from me? This is the answer to my prayers then, my Lord?"

I stare up at the face of Christ, rake my gaze across His features frozen in agony.

"Tell me, my Lord, is this the way You repay me for the years I spent in Your service, in making sure I did everything that was my duty to You, in ensuring that I would leave no stone unturned in my loyalty to You? It was all a test, wasn't it? Every single thing I did has led up to this moment, and I am helpless to stop it. For I am not in control... You are...or so You'd have me think?" I tip up my chin glare at He who does not speak to me anymore.

"Well, guess what? Not anymore. From this day on, I am no longer in Your service. No one controls my destiny. Not him—" I stab my finger in the direction of the figure on the ground, "not You, not anyone else. Me, I am the master of my destiny. Me, Edward Chase, from here on, I renounce my association with You."

The wind blows in through the open side door, which slams shut. The sound ricochets around the space, coils into my guts. "Oh, no, you don't." I smile up at the figure on the wall. "You can't stop me, not now. You had Your chance and You lost it. You lost me, my Lord. This is where we part ways."

I snatch the collar from around my neck and drop it on the man on the floor.

Then walk out the side door, through the garden, to my cottage. I pick up my phone, stare at it, then dial the one number I'd sworn never to call.

# 24

---

*"Earbuds firmly stuck in her ears, my mum dances around the lawn, backlit against the sinking sun. Her weights are in her hands, swinging dangerously near to her head every time she raises her arms. She's supposedly working out, and as she launches into the chorus of Prince's Purple Rain, I can see her face light up."*
-From Ava's diary

Ava

Thunder booms outside and I sit up with a gasp. It's dark in the room and I reach for my lamp and flick it on. The light illuminates the room but doesn't dispel the unease that gathers in the pit of my belly. I snatch up my phone, check the time. It's two am, the dead of night. Goosebumps pop on my skin. I rub my hands together, blow on them, then stare at the band-aid Edward had placed on the scraped skin at the base of my palm. I peel off the bandage, find the wound is already half healed. That didn't take long. Some gashes heal quickly. Others — well, others only fester over time.

A shudder runs down my spine.

It's freezing and not even being under three duvets is keeping me warm. Ugh. The temperature must have plummeted outside, as it sometimes does in London. It was sunny yesterday, the warmest day in March for the last fifty years, or so the media headlines had proclaimed. Which is why, no doubt, the mercury dropped the other way today. I roll up the bandage toss it into the wastebasket near the bedside table. Just then, lightning flashes outside. Rain patters against the window at the same time that the doorbell rings.

Huh? Who can it be? I'm not expecting any of the girls to come by, and anyway, they'd never drop by unannounced. In the middle of the night. I pick up the phone and check my messages. Nope, nothing.

The doorbell rings again, then someone bangs against the door.

I stiffen, clutch my phone in my hand like it's a weapon. Shit, I don't have anything to defend myself with. But thieves don't ring doorbells, do they? *Not unless they want to take you by surprise when you opened the door.* My pulse rate ratchets up. I slip out of the bed and the cold wraps around me. I shiver, walk to the kitchen, glance around, then grab the first thing I find. A wooden spoon. Shit, that's not going to help.

The banging on the door resumes again, and I pivot, walk toward it and peer through the keyhole.

Golden eyes glare back at me. I gulp; my fingers tremble. The phone slips from my hand and hits the floor. Shit, shit, shit. I snatch it up, then juggling the wooden spoon and the phone in one hand, I open the door to find Edward framed in the doorway.

"Wha...what are you doing here?" I gulp.

He rakes his gaze down my features, to where I'm holding the phone and wooden spoon, then back to my face.

His hair is mussed, droplets of water dot his face, trail down his beautiful throat, down the demarcation between those sculpted pecks. Goosebumps pop on my skin for a second time in a few minutes, this time for completely different reasons. I rub one bare foot over the other and he jerks his gaze down my chest, to my hips, to my bare legs. Shit. In my hurry to get a weapon, I'd forgotten to wear something warmer, so I'm still clad in my camisole and the knickers that I'd worn to bed.

His nostrils flare. He glances up, meets my gaze. His irises blaze a gorgeous golden. I see myself reflected in them and shiver. Thunder cracks outside again and I jump. The phone slips from my hand. Again. He swoops down, grabs it before it hits the ground, then straightens. "Invite me in," he commands.

"Wh…what?"

"Ask me in, Eve," he snaps. "Now."

I gulp. "W…won't you come in?" I take a step back, then skitter to the side as he brushes past me. The scent of freshly cut grass mixed with rain envelops me. My nipples harden and my thighs clench. Moisture pools between my legs. Shit, at this rate I am going to dampen my panties and he's going to know the effect he has on me, considering I have no clothes to hide behind.

The wind picks up outside again, and I close the door. I turn to find him standing in the center of the living room. He seems to have absorbed all the oxygen in the room, for I try to breathe, but my lungs burn. I try to swallow but my throat is too dry. Hell. Why does he have this effect on me? I take a trembling step forward, then another. He must hear the slight noise I make, for he tenses. He drops his backpack to the floor, then shrugs off his leather jacket and tosses it aside. His shoulders flex, the defined planes of his back outlined against the shirt that pulls tightly across his torso.

He raises a hand to run his fingers through his hair, and the action outlines his biceps, which bulge and flex. A hot flare of desire pools low in my belly. My thighs spasm, my palms dampen, and I rub them across my thighs. I rake my gaze down that delicious butt of his, those powerful thighs clad in jeans. He's also wearing biker boots. Proper shit-kickers. I've never seen him wear those before. For that matter, I've never seen him in jeans either. I lower my gaze, to the backpack at his feet.

"Are you going somewhere?" I frown.

"I came to see you." He pivots to face me and the force of his intense gaze slams into my chest. A shudder grips me. I tighten my grip around the wooden spoon I'm still holding in my hand. His gaze darts to that, then back to me. "Do you want me to use that?"

"What?" I blink at him. "What do you mean?"

"Do you," he takes a step forward, "want me," another step and another, "to use that," he stops a few inches in front of me, "on you?"

Heat flushes my skin. He's not. He can't be... Is he saying what I think he is?

"You mean..." I gulp, "you want to..."

"Spank you?" He tilts his head. "Do you?"

*Yes.*

*Yes.*

"No," I squeak, then clear my throat. "Wh...what are you doing here?"

"That's not important. What is, is that I am here. I came to see you, Ava." He drags his hand through his hair again and I notice his fingers tremble. Huh? Is he nervous? No, he's not nervous... This is something else. I peer into his features, notice the skin pulled tightly across his cheek bones. There are fine lines around his eyes, which I swear I haven't noticed before. He looks on edge, strung tight, like he's about to do something...or has done something that's not in the normal scheme of things. Considering the time and his arrival on my doorstep.

"What happened?" I scowl at him. "What have you done, Edward?"

He stares at me, then chuckles. He peels back his lips and laughs, and the sound is harsh and ugly and so pain-filled that I wince.

I take a step forward. "Ed, what's wrong?"

He firms his lips, looks me up and down, before kicking his bag aside, his movements barely restrained. The backpack hits the wall, the sound a soft thud that reverberates through my blood. My pulse skitters; the blood pounds at my temples.

"Ed?" I tilt my head, "What do you want?"

"You," he bites out the word, "I want you."

## 25

Ava

The tone of his voice slices through the thoughts in my mind. It coils around my breasts, slithers down to nestle between my legs. I shiver. "B...but...your vows."

"Fuck my vows."

I blink. A part of me rejoices. Yes, yes. This is what I wanted to hear. This is what I've been hoping for since I first met him... so... Why am I not jumping for joy? Why am I not throwing myself at him, winding my arms around his neck, locking my legs around his waist and dry humping myself on the tent in his crotch?

"Edward?" I stiffen, "What's wrong?"

"What's wrong is that you are still dressed."

"And you're not..." I stare at his throat, "you're not wearing your collar."

"I won't be needing it anymore."

"What does that mean?" I scowl.

"You don't get to ask the questions," he growls. "Which reminds me, why are we still standing here?"

"What do you mean?"

He closes the distance between us, so the heat from his body slams into my chest. "Do you or do you not want me to fuck you, Ava?"

My core clenches. My toes curl. All of my nerve-endings seem to light up. Jesus—and it is okay to use his name, since we're not standing in a church, right? This man... The power he has over me... It'll never go away, not until the day I die. Not even then. Bet he'll haunt me in my afterlife and chase me through the catacombs of hell, which is clearly where I am going, considering I tempted one of God's most faithful disciples.

"What have I done to you, Ed?" I tip up my chin, stare into those brilliant brown eyes of his.

"Are you done?" he grates out through clenched teeth. "I am asking you for the last time, Ava, do you want me to shag you or not?"

I draw in a sharp breath, then nod my head.

"I didn't hear you," he growls.

"Y...yes," I whimper.

"Say it like you mean it, Eve."

"Yes," I snap. "Yes, yes, ye—"

He thrust his thumb inside my mouth. "Suck on it," he orders, and I curl my tongue around his digit. The saltiness of his skin, combined with that edgy, darkness that is pure Edward sinks into my blood. My pussy spasms. Moisture trickles down the inside of my legs.

He darts his gaze down to my crotch as if he can see right through my panties. I'm pretty sure he can't. Bet he senses it, though. He's always known what he does to me. How helpless I am in the face of his commands. All he has to do is ask and I'll lay myself down at his feet, legs apart, asking him to wreck me.

A moan bleeds from my lips. He jerks his chin up, his gaze alert, watching me, assessing me, stalking my every single movement. I freeze, not wanting to give myself away... Well, not more than what I have revealed so far, that is. Shit, at this rate, I am not going to last. I am going to orgasm just being in his presence... Yep, totally possible when it's Edward. The man exudes enough testosterone that just being close to him has heightened the senses of every single cell in my body.

He stares at my mouth with such intensity that a shudder ladders down my spine. I squeeze my thighs together and he scowls. "Stop fidgeting."

He drags his thumb down my chin, down my throat to the valley between my breasts. "You're so fucking beautiful, Ava." His words are complimentary but his tone... It's brooding. Almost angry. His eyebrows slash down and he hooks his finger in the neckline and tugs. The thin cloth tears down the middle.

I gasp, look down to find the two halves gape enough to expose the sides of my breasts. The fabric catches on my nipples and stays there.

"Fuck me," he growls. "The things I want to do to you, Eve. If only I had more time."

"What do you mean? We have time. You only just got here, you —"

"Shh," he raises his finger back to my lips, "any last requests, Eve?"

I gulp; my fingers tremble. Shit, that sounds dangerous and surprising and so bloody hot.

"L...last, requests?" I manage to squeak.

He cups my cheek, stares into my eyes, "Once I bury myself inside of you, you won't be doing any talking. Hell, I'm going to make sure I fuck you so hard, and in every hole in your body, in such quick succession that your brain cells are going to be out of commission for a while..." he explains in a matter-of-fact voice.

It's so different from his normal tone that I stare at him. "Is e... everything okay, Ed?"

"Everything is not okay, Eve," he explains patiently. "You are still standing and coherent." He shakes his head. "We need to change that."

"We...we do?"

He nods.

"Turn around and put your hands against up the wall," he orders.

"What?" I blink.

"Don't ask me to repeat myself. You won't like the consequences."

"I... I won't?"

He shakes his head.

"Do it, Eve." His gaze narrows. "Now."

I turn, head for the wall, then stop and stare at him over my shoulder. "My phone?" I manage to force out the words. "What about my phone?"

"This?" He takes it from me, stares at it. "You won't be needing this for a while." He tosses it over his shoulder.

I squeak, then exhale a sigh of relief when it lands on the couch.

He prowls toward me, circles the air with his finger.

I scowl.

He glares at me and I shiver.

He arches an eyebrow and I bite down the inside of my cheek. Shit, this...whatever mood he is in, is hot. Only... Something is different. I haven't known Edward long enough, but one thing I've always believed in, that I could trust him. This...this man standing in my living room... There's a sense of desperation, a ruthlessness that... feels right. Yeah, it feels right, and yet, it's also disconcerting. It's as if he's peeled back a layer, the mask that he wears to the world, to reveal the wolf beneath...the wolf in sheep's clothing. Yeah, he was always alpha, even—perhaps especially—dressed in his priest's garb. But this version of Ed? This snarling, growling, jeans and shit-kickers garbed Ed... It's a whole new level. A person I have no hope of trying to control. Not that I want to... But also, I don't want to give in and do as he says. I mean... I'm not one to just be commanded... Though I like it, I want it, yearn for it. But I also want to be conquered. Know what I mean?

I turn to face the wall, raise my hands, then realize I'm still holding the goddamn wooden spoon in my hand. "Oh." I stare at it, and he reaches over my shoulder, plucks the weapon—I mean, utensil—from my grasp. Shit, now I feel truly naked. I mean, I still have some clothes on, but now I have nothing to defend myself with. Not that I want to defend myself against this guy...but... Yeah, shit, now I really am at his mercy.

"Ed?" I whisper and he shushes me.

"No talking, Eve."

"But—"

*Whack.* The back of the wooden spoon connects with my butt.

"What the—?" I screech. "Did you just spank me with that—?"

*Whack, whack, whack.* He hits my arse in quick succession with that freakin' wooden spoon and pinpricks of pain radiate from my backside. My core spasms. Moisture pools between my legs and I press my forehead into the wall. Damn it, this should not arouse me. Should not. Really shouldn't. But I am turned on. No denying. What's wrong with me?

I turn my head, scowl at him over my shoulder.

He slaps the wooden spoon against his palm, and the soft thud sends a shiver racing down my spine again. He tilts his head, holds my gaze, then nods as if satisfied.

"I assume you still want me to fuck you?"

I frown.

"Say no, and I'll leave," he adds.

I blink. Why is he doing this? Is he giving me another way out? Why did he barge in, in the middle of the night? Is he on his way somewhere? He is, that's for sure. So why has he stopped here first? Did he miss me? Maybe. Does he want me? Yes. Does he need me? Definitely. It's why he came by. Whether he knows it or not, he seeks comfort— No, he needs to give in to whatever is tearing him apart inside. Something he is not ready to share, something that's shaken him enough to turn his back on his vows, his life-long pursuit of discipline, of the framework within which he's lived his life, and come to me. And I can't turn him away, I can't. More to the point, I need him as much as he needs me. If this is the only way I am going to have him, then so be it.

I nod my head.

The breath rushes out of him. "Say it aloud."

"Yes."

His eyes gleam. Something like satisfaction laces his features. "I'm going to take your mouth, and tear into your pussy, then I'm going to fuck you in the arse. You'll let me do that, won't you sweet Eve?"


Ava

His filthy words send a surge of heat through my veins. My pulse rate skyrockets. My knees wobble, and if I hadn't had my palms pressed into the wall, I swear I'd have collapsed by now. Who'd have thought the straight-talking Father Edward Chase has a dirty mouth on him? I stare up into his face, and his nostrils flare.

"Say yes, Eve," he growls. "Say you want me to take you in every hole. Tell me you want me to fuck you wherever I choose. Do it," he snaps, his tone half belligerent, half pleading. "Do it, Eve, you have my permission to speak."

I rake my gaze across his tense features, his flexed shoulders, the hard set of his stance as he stands there, watching me, waiting for me to tell him that it is okay for him to fuck me in the arse. Shit. I squeeze my eyes shut. Once I say yes, there is no going back. Once he has his hands and his mouth on me and his fingers inside of me, I'll be branded as his. He'll have spoiled me for everyone else. I'll never be able to look at another man and not feel Edward's touch, his kisses, the force of his presence, the strength of his attraction, the pull of that something inside of him, which is just so carnal yet so pure, so single-minded and intense that there could be no space for anyone else in my heart, my mind, my...soul. Only he can reduce me to this mass of quivering need that propels me to take the leap. That spurs me on to open my eyes, look him in the eyes and say, "Yes."

The breath rushes out of him. He flings the wooden spoon aside, closes the space between us and kicks my legs further apart. Then, he leans in close enough for his body heat to envelop me. His big body looms over me as he presses his nose into my hair and inhales deeply. A ripple runs down his body and I know then just how affected he is by his proximity to me, as well.

"You smell so bloody good, Eve," he rumbles. He nuzzles into the curve between my ear and my neck, then runs his tongue around the shell of my ear and sucks my earlobe. My core clenches and moisture trickles down my thigh.

A groan bleeds out of me and he shudders. He presses his body into mine and the hardness of his arousal digs into the curve of my arse.

"F-u-c-k," he growls against my hair, then air hits my back. I glance over my shoulder to find he's dropped down to his knees, between my legs. My throat closes. He hooks his finger under the waistband of my panties and tugs. The delicate material snaps and he whips it off of me. He stuffs it in his pocket, then shoves his shoulders between my thighs, forcing me to part them further. He grips my hips, then lowers his head and swipes his tongue up my melting pussy.

Heat sweeps up my spine and the blood rushes to my face. Ohmigod. What the hell is he doing? How are his movements so sure, so focused? He's done this before. Of course, he has. No other way, could he know his way around a woman's body so well—oh! — He stabs his tongue inside my channel, in-out-in, and I throw back my head and pant.

He curls his tongue inside my core, slides his hand between my pussy and the wall and circles my clit with his fingers. I snap back my shoulders, simultaneously push against the wall and thrust my hips forward, riding the thrust of that wicked tongue, chasing the drumming of his fingers across my pussy lips. He brings his other hand up to cup my butt, then slides his thumb in between my arsecheeks and inside my puckered hole.

He continues to tongue-fuck me, while grinding his heel into my clit and sliding his thumb deeper inside my backhole.

Heaven help me.

Where did Father learned to eat out a woman like this?

The tremors sweep up my legs, coil in my center, then surge up my spine. I slap my palms into the wall, squeeze my eyes shut and give in to the orgasm that tears through me.

It seems to go on and on, then fades away as suddenly. I slump back, trembling. Sweat beads my shoulders and my back, my knees tremble, and my thighs spasm, unable to hold me up. The next second, the world tilts. I crack my eyelids open to find that I am on my back, on the floor, with Edward looming over me.

"I am going to fuck you now."

His words slice through the noise in my head. I stare up at him as he reaches down and releases the zipper on his jeans. He shoves his hand into his briefs pulling himself out and pumps, once, twice, thrice. I gaze down at his long, thick, hard, length. It's gorgeous. Almost as beautiful as the man himself. Not that I have seen many cocks, not in real life, at least. Hello Pornhub, you've had your uses, but you have nothing on this one-hundred percent virile specimen who sits back on his heels, between my thighs. He slides his hand between us, scoops up the cum from my slit, and slathers it into my backhole.

*No.* I shake my head and clench my buttcheeks.

"Shh." He lowers his head to mine, brushes his mouth over mine, once, twice. I part my lips and he slides his tongue inside, tangles with mine. He sucks on me, draws from me. He groans into my mouth and I swear it feels like he's poured himself into his kiss. All of him. I taste myself on his breath, breathe in the lingering scent of frankincense, and under that, the familiar cut grass scent that is him.

It's so familiar, so reassuring that I relax.

My muscles unwind. I loop my arms about his neck, return the kiss. I open my mouth wider, tangle my tongue with his, and his big body shudders. I lean up and into him, strain to get closer. He hooks his arms under my knees, pulls them up, only to wind my ankles about his neck.

"Hold on," he growls as he inches his dick into my backhole.

"Oh," I gasp into his mouth, "oh, my."

He doesn't let up. He slides his tongue in and out of my mouth, while he slips a hand between us and curls his fingers around my clit. Heat slices through me; sweat pools under my armpits. Moisture drips from my cunt, as I shudder and dig my fingertips into his shoulders, wrap my ankles more securely about him...wait as he releases my mouth to gaze into my eyes.

"You're so tight," he rasps. "So hot." He thrusts his hips and slips inside further.

*Too much, too full.* "Edward," I gasp, "you're too big."

"I'm just right for you." He slips one thick finger inside my pussy and I shudder. He slides in another and begins to work them in and out of me. In and out.

All the while he holds my gaze, his golden eyes now a dark brown, almost as dark as the skies outside. I tip up my chin and he lowers his lips to mine again. He licks my mouth, presses his thumb into my clit, and curls his fingers inside my channel.

I arch under him, push my breasts up and into his chest, even as I shy away from the coming hurt. "Please," I whimper. "Please, Ed."

"Tell me what you need, Eve." He picks up speed, saws his fingers in and out of me, the wet, squelching sound of my flesh giving in to him filling the space. It's filthy, dirty and oh, so erotic.

The pores of my skin pop and a shudder grips me. My nipples tighten until they ache and my belly quivers. I tilt my hips up and he slides in and through the tight ring of my sphincter. "Oh," I gasp. "Ohmigod, Ed."

"Tell me how it feels," he commands.

"Like..." I swallow, "Like you've crammed yourself into me, like you are consuming me, and now I can never let you go."

A strange look enters his eyes. He glances away, then back at me. The tendons of his throat move as he swallows. "I'm going to have to go away, Eve. I'm going to have to leave."

# 26

Ava

I stare at him, "What, what are you saying, you—?"

He lowers his head and closes his mouth over mine, deepens the kiss, absorbs my words at the same time he begins to move. He pulls out of me, all the way to the edge then propels his hips forward and into me. Pinpricks of pain radiate out and up my spine.

He begins to weave his fingers in and out of me again, as he fills my mouth with his tongue and continues to fuck my arse. He slides out, then in one smooth, long swipe, fills me again. This time he hits a spot somewhere deep inside me that I didn't even know existed. My eyes roll back in my head. My entire body bucks. My shoulders jerk, and I arch under him, try to pull away, even as I want to get closer to him. To crawl under his skin and stay there. To tie myself to him and never let go... He can't go. Why did he say that he has to leave? Why?

I snap my eyes open to find him watching me. He holds my gaze as he plunges forward again and again, each time hitting that same spot, and I can't take it anymore. The tremors sweep up from my toes, up my legs, my thighs, pool in my center, before they slam up my spine and burst behind my eyes. The climax barrels into me and I yell —but he swallows the sound and keeps fucking me. He curls his fingers inside me, slams into me with such force that my entire body bucks. He thrusts once-twice-thrice then tears his mouth from mine, and with a low shout, empties himself inside me.

He slips his fingers out of my pussy, eases my legs down, then slumps forward, and for a second, his entire weight presses me into the floor. I'm surrounded by his intensely male scent, by the heat of his body, which coalesces with mine, by the sensation of his skin slippery with sweat, sliding over mine.

Then he rolls over and deposits me on his chest.

I press my cheek into the V of skin exposed by his shirt. His heart thunders against my ear, his breathing a ragged melody that soothes me and reminds me once more about what he said.

I place my chin in the demarcation between his pecs, stare up into his face, "Don't go." The words rasp out and I swallow. "I don't know what happened earlier, but whatever it is, we can face it together."

He stares down at me. "Why do you think something happened?"

"Didn't it?"

"It doesn't matter." He grips my shoulders and I know he's going to push me off of him. He's going to set me aside, get dressed, pick up his bag and leave and I… I cannot allow that. My heart begins to race; the blood thuds at my temple. I sit up, wince when my backside twinges, both from the spanking and from where he'd taken me, but I don't care. I rise to my feet, hold out my hand.

He frowns. "What are you doing?"

"Come with me," I snap.

He scowls. "You don't tell me what to do."

"Oh?" I glower back. "I just let you take my arse, you asshole. The least you can do is humor me for a little while longer."

The furrow between his eyebrows deepens, he hesitates, and I add, "You owe me this much."

He looks like he's about to protest, then jerks his chin. He ignores my hand, and pushes up to tower over me.

I turn, head inside, through my bedroom, and into the ensuite, where I flick on the light switch. Pulling off my torn camisole I step into the shower cubicle, turn on the shower, then turn to find him watching me from the doorway.

I jerk my head toward the running water, and he frowns.

He opens his mouth to say something, then decides against it. Instead, he stalks over, at the same time reaching behind to tear off his shirt. I take in the expanse of his chest, those perfect pecs, the eight—no, ten-pack—shit, when does Father have the time to work out? He pulls off his boots and socks, then shoves down his pants and his boxers, kicking them aside. He straightens and his cock juts up. It seems even bigger, thicker, if that's possible, considering he was just inside me. The head is swollen, and glistening from his cum, and a vein runs up the underside. Moisture pools in my mouth and I swallow, force myself to lower my gaze past those powerful thighs, to his corded calves and the wide feet that move toward me. He brushes past me, steps into the shower and raises his head to the flow of water. The space instantly seems to shrink, not that it was big to start, but with this six-foot, three-inch behemoth in the cubicle which had been perfectly big enough for me, there's barely enough space for me to slide around and in front of him.

He watches me with a narrowed gaze as I reach out and pour some of the soap into my palm. Then I wash his chest, run my hands down those sculpted pecs, down his hard stomach, circle around the hard shaft which twitches as I sink to my knees and wash his thighs, his feet. I tip my chin up, survey him through the downpour. Water drops cling to his cheeks, spike his eyelashes, flatten his hair so it outlines the shape of his skull. There are hollows under his cheekbones and dark circles ring his eyes. How had I not noticed them before? What happened to make him break his vows? To make him want to leave so suddenly.

*Leave. He wants to leave. Not yet. Not if I can help it.*

I reach up, curl my fingers around his thick shaft. My fingers barely meet around his girth. Fuck me. How the hell had I taken him, and in my arse, at that? It is going to hurt like hell tomorrow. Only, I am not going to stop there. I wrap my other palm around his dick, then swipe up.

He hisses out a breath. His gaze intensifies. His massive chest rises and falls, as he parts his legs, giving me better access. I rise up on my knees, continue to pump him, up-down-up, and his flesh hardens, lengthens, throbs in my grasp.

His stomach muscles clench, his jaw ticks, and a nerve throbs at his temple. He slams a hand out and into the wall, and his biceps flex as he takes in a deep breath, then another.

I balance myself with one palm on his thigh and he flinches. His muscles coil, his shoulders flex, then a growl rips out of him.

He grits his teeth, holding my gaze as I increase the pace of my movements. His cock jumps in my grasp and he bares his teeth. "What are you waiting for?" he growls. "Suck me off."

# 27

Edward

*Suck me off?* Did you just ask her to suck you off? And after you tore into her arse without prepping her properly? Without giving her enough warning? Why the hell did I come here in the first place? I should have left after making that call, and that had been my plan. I had gathered up the very basic essentials I'd need to survive and then I'd mounted my bike and left. I hadn't looked back. Hadn't mourned the remnants of what the last five years of my life had been reduced to. The rectory had been just a space in which my physical body had spent the nights. My time had been taken up by my connection to the Lord, one which I had severed.

And it had hurt. More than when I had left my life behind to join the Church. More than when I had been taken and abused. More than when I had gone on a drug-induced bender and almost died and been reluctantly brought back to the land of the living. Is this what people face when they lose a loved one? Or when they go through a divorce? A separation, a severing of a limb, a loss of something that had been tangible, but which had since—poof! — disappeared like it had never existed at all. Five years of a presence that had occupied my life, my mind, my soul. All of it, gone in an instant. Leaving behind the dregs of a man I don't recognize anymore.

I had straddled my bike, hit the road, and almost not been surprised when I'd landed at her apartment. I'd known I was coming here, even before I'd left. The one place I had pretended didn't exist. The one woman I'd tried so hard to ignore. The only person I could turn to, to fill the gnawing emptiness that permeates my soul.

How could I even try to go on, when the most important parts of me have been left behind? When the only thing that had anchored me has been cut loose, leaving me adrift?

Is that why I had come here…in a final attempt to try to salvage something for myself? Am I that selfish that I would fuck her, claim her, give her hope…when I have nothing to offer to myself anymore?

I should leave. I should spare her further pain. I should simply get out of here, out of her life, before I do something that will hurt her even more.

I gaze down into those emerald green eyes that stare up at me with defiance. With lust. With the kind of devotion that I had once reserved for my Lord, and I know then, it's already too late. For her. For me. For what I am going to do. Which is going to haunt me for the rest of my days. *Get the hell away from her, you bastard. Give her a chance to come out of this unscathed.*

I squeeze my eyes shut and pray—pray—to whom? Not to Him. Not when I've lost my faith, when I've rejected Him. I've lost the very foundation upon which I have built my entire life. Fucking hell. How the hell am I going to walk away from her as well?

She cups my balls and squeezes, and I shudder. I open my eyes to find her rising to her knees. She bends her head, opens her mouth around my cock. I watch as my shaft disappears down her throat. The blood rushes to my groin and my dick thickens further, if that's possible. She pulls out, then licks the crown of my shaft, before taking me in again. The heat, the swirling of her tongue up my length, the scrape of her teeth on the underside of my shaft... All of it converges, coalesces into a hard knot that intensifies, tightens, lodges at the base of my spine.

My thigh muscles tighten and my shoulders tense. I lower my hand, dig my fingers into her hair and tug. Her head falls back, saliva drools from the corners of her mouth and the last bit of sanity seems to leave me.

I tighten my grip on her strands, pull her back, so my dick slides out, until I'm poised at the edge of her lips.

Her gaze widens, her grasp on my balls intensifies, and I can't stop the smirk that twists my lips.

"You want me to fuck you again, is that it? Is that why you stopped me from leaving?"

The green of her irises deepens and color smears her cheeks.

"Maybe you want to tell the world that the hot priest shagged you. Is that why you have my cock in your mouth?"

A low snarl bleeds from her lips. She tries to pull back, but I hold her in place.

"Oh, no, you don't." I widen my smile. "You stopped me when I would have walked away. The least you can do is let me fuck your mouth," I pull her head forward and feed my dick to her, "first."

She chokes and more spit drools down her chin. She stares at me, her gaze hot and angry and filled with lust. Oh, yeah, this thing between us... It is carnal and base... And hell, if it isn't the only thing keeping me tethered to this moment. The present. It's all I have. It's all I'll allow myself to have. There can be no future for us. Not after what I have done. I am better off leaving her, giving her the chance at a normal life with someone else. Someone who isn't me. Not me. *F-u-c-k!*

"Breathe through your nose, Eve." I growl, and she flares her nostrils. Then sucks in her cheeks and the suction, fuck me... The action sets a storm of lust raging through my guts.

I hold onto the wall for support, then begin to pull her head back and forth, back and forth. She releases her grip on my balls, digs her fingertips into my thigh with enough force to send pinpricks of pain racing up my spine. The coiled pressure in my groin grows and grows until it seems to consume all of me, yet I don't stop. I continue to fuck her mouth, pull her forward and back, again and again. The moisture glistens on her cheeks and her breasts heave, the nipples pebbled and pink-tipped and gleaming in the light.

My mouth waters. I tear my gaze from her tits back to her mouth, up to her eyes, now glazed with desire and the need to come. But I am not going to let her. Not yet.

I tug on her hair and a low moan bleeds from her throat.

I increase the speed of my actions, pulling her forward and back, and her entire body jolts. Her breathing speeds up. She squeezes my thigh, widens her gaze, then scrapes her teeth on the underside of my shaft. And that's when the knot of pressure at the base of my spine explodes.

# 28

Ava

His features contort, he throws back his head, and with a muted roar, shoots his load down my throat. His orgasm seems to go on and on and I watch, entranced, as his big body shudders. His shoulders draw in and his massive chest heaves. His cheeks are flushed, the hollows under his cheeks are more prominent. He seems like a man in the throes of emotional turmoil, a man who is at the end of his tether.

The musky, peaty taste of his cum explodes on my palate, and I swallow and suck on him. Damn him, but the sight of him falling apart is burned into my brain. It's something I'll never forget. This power over him, this sense of control that infuses me, turns me on. I slide my hand around to squeeze his butt, then slip my finger in between his arsecheeks to tease his puckered hole.

His entire body jerks.

He lowers his head, locking his gaze with mine, then tugs on my hair. His dick slips out, and he urges me up to my feet.

"Not had enough, Eve?" He thrusts his face into mine, "What the hell do you want from me?"

"The same thing you want from me."

"Want me to fuck you properly, is that it?"

"Finally." I chuckle, the sound harsh. "Took you long enough to get the memo."

A snarl twists his lips and a rush of fear courses through my veins. *Shit, shit, shit. What is wrong with me? Why am I pushing him? Why am I taunting him further, when he already seems to have lost control?*

He releases my hair, only to wrap his fingers around the nape of my neck. He pulls me up to my tiptoes, my skull resting on his fingertips. I raise my eyes, meet his burning gaze. The breath rushes out of me. The lust in his eyes, the anguish, the helplessness... It's as if he hates himself, but can't stop himself from what he is going to do, and for a minute, I feel sorry for him.

His fingers meet in the front of my throat and when he increases the pressure on my nape, my breath hitches.

I part my lips and he lowers his head until his nose bumps mine. Our breaths mingle and the thud-thud-thud of my heartbeat fills my ears. I hold his gaze as he opens his mouth over mine. He slips his tongue in between my lips, tangles it with mine. Pinpricks of heat vibrate from the contact. My chest tightens and a ball of emotion clogs my throat. For some reason, this feels very intimate, more than all of the previous times he's kissed me. Maybe it's because he has his eyes open, and I can take in the sparks of silver that flash in them. He tilts his head and deepens the kiss. I raise my hand and he grabs my wrist, bringing it up above my head, and holds it there, then presses his chest against mine. He thrusts his thigh between my legs and I part them. I wind my other hand about his shoulder, hold on as he thrusts his hips forward and his hard shaft digs into my belly.

A groan rolls up my throat and he swallows it. I slide my hand between us, my fingertips graze the crown of his cock, and he hisses against my mouth. I wrap my fingers around it and his chest heaves. He breaks the kiss to stare into my eyes as I begin to pump him up and down, up and down. His nostrils flare. He releases his hold on my neck and hand, then bends and grabs me under my thighs. He lifts me up and I squeak, wind my legs around his waist. He reaches behind me to shut off the shower, then walks out of the cubicle. He lowers me to the ground, reaches around me to grab a towel, then proceeds to wipe me down. His movements are brisk, almost impersonal, but the thick length of his cock points to just how aroused he really is. When I am dry, he drags the towel down his body, flings it aside. Then, closing the distance between us, he scoops me up. He walks over to my bed and lowers me onto it. On my back, I watch as he rakes his gaze down my body.

"Spread your legs," he commands, and hell, if I don't come right then. I part my thighs and he stares at my pussy with unconcealed greed. He licks his lips and I swallow. He lowers to the floor between my legs, circles my ankles with his fingers and tugs until my butt is poised at the edge of the bed. He hooks my knees over his shoulders, then lowers his head to my core. He breathes in deeply and my stomach quivers.

"The scent of your pussy..." He draws in another breath and his shoulders heave, "It's pure aphrodisiac. Why did I ever think that I could resist it?" He stares up at me and his eyes gleam. "I'll never forget this, Eve, not as long as I live."

"Wait." I blink, "What do you mean—?" I throw my head back and gasp as he licks up my slit in one long, slow sweep.

"Oh, my god." I groan as he follows that up with another long swipe of his tongue. I jerk my body up and off the mattress. He licks me a third time and my eyes roll back in my head.

"I am ready to break my fast, little Eve, will you feed me?"

He closes his mouth around my pussy and I cry out. He thrusts his tongue inside my aching core. I dig my fingers into the sheets, squeeze my thighs around his head. "Omigod. Omigod," I wail. "Edward, please—"

He brings his hand up to pinch my nipple and I explode. The orgasm crashes over me with no warning. It sweeps up my body, exploding behind my eyes, and I cry out. I shudder as the climax grips me, then ebbs away. I slump. My muscles slacken. He continues to lick my clit, curls his tongue around the swollen nub and I moan. "Please" I whisper, "please, Ed."

He rises up, forcing me to open my legs further. The bed dips as he lowers his weight onto his elbows and brackets me in. The heat from his body slams into my chest, coils around me, pours into my skin and heats my blood. He peers deep into my eyes. "Do you still want me?"

"Yes," I moan. "Fuck me, Ed."

A fierce look heats his eyes. Those golden eyes blaze, mirrored pools of desire in which I can see myself, see my lust reflected in how his breathing intensifies. His nostrils flare. He reaches down to position his dick at my entrance then pauses. "Condom," he growls. "I need a condom."

"Oh." I blink, try to pull my thoughts together. Of course, we do. I hadn't even considered it, as out of my head with lust as I am. "I... I don't have any."

He frowns. "I'm clean." His lips twist.

Of course, he is, he's been celibate for as long as he's been a priest. And he's going to break his abstinence with me. I gulp, his scowl intensifies. He tilts his head and I realize he's waiting for me to speak. What...what was it I was going to say?

"Eve?" He prompts, "I said I'm clean."

"Uh, I... I am clean too." I blink rapidly. "Also, I am on the pill." I've actually been on the pill for years due to my irregular periods. Of course, it had crossed my mind that this meant if Ed made love to me, there wouldn't need to be any barriers between us. I confess though that I didn't think that it could actually happen. My breath catches, as the enormity of the situation sinks in. OMG, Edward's here and he's going to fuck me... Without a condom.

His shoulders flex and his biceps seem to bulge. "Good," he rumbles as he lowers himself between my knees.

Leaning over, he cups my cheek, then kisses me. He tilts his head, brushes his lips over mine again and again. He kisses me with such tenderness that my heart trembles and my toes curl. I flutter my eyelids down, wind my arms about his neck and open my mouth, my body, my heart to him.

"You ready?" he whispers, and his hot breath sears my mouth.

I nod, and he positions himself against my slit. The crown of his dick nudges my opening, and I draw in a breath. Oh, my god, it's happening. It's really, really happening. Edward is going to make love to me. I swallow, and he must sense my sudden panic because he brushes my mouth with his. "Shh, don't worry. I'll take care of you, Eve."

I gaze up at him. "You...you will?"

He nods. "Do you trust me?"

I pause.

"Do you?" He holds my gaze. "Do you, Eve?"

I swallow again, then nod.

"Say it then," he commands.

"I... I trust you, Edward."

A smile curves his lips. "Then promise me you won't believe what you'll hear about me."

"Hear about you?" I scowl. "What do you—?"

He pushes forward and breaches me.

"Oh!" Pain radiates out from my core and I gasp.

He freezes. "The hell?" His gaze seems to clear and his features twist. "Are you a virgin, Eve?"

## 29

Edward

She blinks and color smears her cheeks. Fuck me, it's not possible. She is young, but not that young. She is nineteen. Don't most women these days lose their virginity much earlier? Thanks to the confessions I've heard, I know that to be true. Not that I'd ever share it with anyone. Not even now that I am walking away from the priesthood. But still. Ava, a virgin?

"Answer me." I lower my voice to a hush, "Are you, a virgin, Eve?"

She nods. "I should have told you, but I didn't want to scare you away."

I squeeze my eyes shut. My dick lengthens further inside her, the thickness grazing against her soft, melting, warmth. My balls tighten and my thigh muscles spasm. She was a virgin. I was her first. Something fierce grips my chest. I shouldn't have come here... And yet, I wouldn't trade this for anything else in the world.

And I am going to leave her after taking her virginity? Goddamn it, this isn't fair. Not to her. Not to me. Of course, He had to orches-

trate it this way, to make sure I would carry the memory of her sweet-
ness, her warm, wet pussy that clamps around my dick, her virgin
cunt that no one has had before. I am her first. And damn, if I am
going to let anyone else take what is mine after this. I have to find a
way to return. I will find a way to come back. No way, am I going to
stay away from her after this. I lower my forehead to hers. "You
should have," I agree, "and it would have ensured that I stayed far
away from you."

"And now?" she whispers.

"Now, nothing will keep us apart, Eve."

"Then why are you not following through with your word?"

I lean back, balance my weight on my arms. "What do you mean?"

"Why are you not fucking me like you mean it?"

I can't stop the chuckle that rips up my throat.

This woman. The things she says.

"I don't want to hurt you." I lower my head and rub her nose with
mine. "It's your first time. I'd rather take it slow."

"I'd rather that you fuck me the way I want you to."

She tilts up her hips and I slide further inside her soaking wet
channel. The heat, the warmth, the way her pussy clamps down on my
dick, and it's like I am coming home. My heart stutters. My pulse
pounds at my temples. The blood drains to my groin and my cock
thickens inside of her. She gasps, tips up her chin. Those green eyes
widen with surprise, with lust, with a tenderness that sparks off an
answering heat in my chest. My belly knots. My dick throbs inside of
her. I want to own her, to brand her, to possess her, to make her mine.
To ensure she doesn't forget me during the time I am gone.

*Does that make me selfish, God? Does that make me the kind of sinner
whom You'll never forgive? Oh, wait. I don't need Your approval anymore. I can
do whatever the fuck I want.*

"Edward."

My name on her lips, the scent of her trapped in my skin, the
feel of her legs wrapped around my waist. The heat of her pussy
enveloping my dick. Fuck me, but I've died and gone to heaven. Or
hell... And what a hell this is... One of my own making. One where
I have never felt more, sensed more, heard more. One I can feel

with every pore in my body. I touch my forehead to hers. "The things you make me do, Eve. You drive me out of my head, you know that?"

"That makes two of us." She reaches up, runs her fingers through my hair. "Please." She swallows. "Please make love to me."

My throat closes. My limbs tremble and something hot stabs at my chest. "I can do that, my darling Eve. I can give you this to remember me by."

"Remember you by?" She gulps. "Why do you keep saying tha—?"

I push forward, and my dick slips in further.

"Edward," she whines. "It's too much. I am too full, I—"

"Shh." I lower my head, brush my lips over hers. "You're beautiful, Eve, and it's not just your body I'm talking about. It's who you are. It's the goodness in you. That purity of your soul that attracted me to you."

"I... It did?" She glances away.

"I saw you and knew there was something different about you. I knew you were going to be trouble, then."

"You did?"

I nod. "What I didn't count on was how much you'd occupy my thoughts."

"Same." Her lips tremble. "I couldn't get you out of my mind, from the moment I saw you."

Warmth fills my chest. This connection is all I have left. And I am going to have to walk away from it, too. Goddam it. Why did it have to turn out this way?

"What's wrong?" she whispers.

"Nothing." I pull out of her, then push forward, sliding in even further this time.

"Oh," she gasps again, then digs her heels into my back. She pushes up and into me and I grip her hip.

"Easy." I smirk. "I don't want you to be sore."

She snorts. "A bit late for that."

"So sassy." I scan her features. "You come across so much more grown up than your years, that it's easy to forget sometimes that you are only nineteen."

"Old soul." She half smiles. "It's why I am so independent; I've always been self-reliant."

"I wish..." *I could be there for you,* is what I want to say. Instead, I thrust my hips forward, ease myself inside her.

Her entire body jolts. "Oh." Her eyelids flutter. "Oh, Edward."

"When you say my name like that," I grit out, "it kills me, Eve. You know that?"

She peers up at me from under her eyelashes. "What else do I do to you?"

"You fishing for compliments?" I mock scowl.

She bites down on her lower lip. "You ready to give me compliments?"

"Always." I brace myself on my elbows, allow her to adjust to my size. Slowly, slowly... A bit late for that, though, considering how I had taken her arse earlier. "If I'd known..." I swallow, "If I'd realized that you were a virgin —"

"You wouldn't have come at all," she completes my statement.

I rake my gaze across her features and she blows out a breath.

"It's why I didn't tell you. There were enough barriers between us, as it was. Add to that, I was a virgin, and I knew you'd never give this," she gestures between us, "whatever this is between us, a chance."

"You should have told me, Eve."

"I don't regret it." She sets her jaw.

I purse my lips, not wanting to reveal what is on my mind. How can I? When she has given me something so unexpected. Something that affects me so deeply... But I cannot let that stop me. I need to put distance between myself and what I had done. I need time to work out what I want to do in life. It's not fair on her that I stay, not when I am so confused about who I am, and what I want for myself. If I am not clear about my path, how can I ever do justice to whatever is there between us?

It's why I need her to believe the worst of me... Fuck me, but I need her to forget that she ever met me. It is the only way I can leave, safe in the knowledge that I am not leaving her hanging in limbo.

No one knows that better than me. The days and nights when I had been taken and kept bound, not knowing if I was going to make it out of there alive... Not seeing the light at the end of the tunnel. That was the worst. I'd never want her to go through that.

I shouldn't have come here, but I did, and now I have to make sure that I complete what I started.

"That's good, I suppose." I smother the voice inside calling me a liar.

"It is?" She frowns.

"Virginity is so overrated anyway."

# 30

Ava

"What?" I stare up at him. "What the hell did you say?"

"You heard me." His lips twist in a smirk that is Edward, and yet, it isn't.

"What do you mean, Ed?"

"I mean..." He pulls out of me, then thrusts forward with just enough force that my entire body jolts. Tendrils of heat shudder out from the impact. My pussy clenches around his dick. Moisture pools in my core and my nipples tighten.

"Oh, god," I groan.

"That too." He stares at me with such burning intensity that my chest tightens. "But what I was going to say is that you had to give up your virginity some time. May as well have been to a man of God, right?"

Something hot stabs at my chest. My vision tunnels. Before I can stop myself, I snake out my palm, which connects with his cheek.

His face snaps back. The thud of the slap echoes around the room.

There's silence. Then thunder rumbles in the distance. Lightning flashes outside. The brightness illuminates his features for a second, highlighting the hollows under his cheekbones, the darkness that rings his eyes. For a second, he looks feral and wild...so unlike the quiet, if dominant, man I've come to know.

But do I? Do I know him at all?

I only met him a week ago and fell for him. I'd known there was more to him than the front he presented to the world, but at that time, I'd put it down to the fact that behind his guise as a priest there was a passionate man, someone who felt so deeply; someone who, when he'd finally admit his feelings for me, would burn me up with his passion.

And right now, watching him, I know I was right all along. Behind that civilized veneer is a beast... someone who I have no clue about, someone I do not know at all.

"Edward—"

"Shut up," he barks.

I gape. "What are you—?"

"I told you to keep quiet, didn't I?" he growls as he pulls out of me, then plunges forward. His dick fills me, stretches me, and his balls slap against my inner thighs. The crown of his cock hits that secret spot deep inside of me and I cry out.

Above me, he tenses, then begins to move. He saws in and out of me, in and out. Each time he pushes in, his shaft hits that spot, again and again. Goosebumps pop on my skin. My nipples tighten into hard nubs of agony, my pussy clenches down on his shaft, and he groans. He tilts his hips, propels forward with enough force that the entire bed frame shakes. The headboard slams into the wall and vibrations of heat and lust shoot up my spine. "Omigod, I am going to—"

"Come for me," he snarls. "Come all over my cock."

His voice shoves me over the edge and I shatter. Moisture gushes out from between my legs and my body bucks. I throw my head back as the climax overwhelms me. When I open my eyes, he's above me, watching me, tracking my every reaction.

I blink at him, watch as the tenderness in his gaze slips away to be replaced by a coldness, a single-minded intent that sends a shiver of apprehension crawling down my spine.

"Edward—"

"Shh." He cups my breast, dragging his thumb across my sensitized nipple. "So, fucking beautiful." His voice is remote, his tone hard. Almost as hard as his shaft that's still inside of me.

"Ed—" I shiver as he hooks his arms behind my knees, shoves them up so they are bent on either side of my chest. I am splayed out, open and vulnerable. A sacrifice on the altar of this priest who seems to have shed the last vestiges of his humanity along with his robe. "Ed, please—"

He shakes his head and I subside. I draw in a shuddering breath, watch as his nostrils flare. His shoulders bunch, then he pulls out of me, stays poised with his cock at the rim of my slit.

"You are going to come again with me."

"No," I beg. "Please, not yet."

"Yes," he insists.

"I can't."

"You will." He pistons forward, and I am so wet, so ready, that he slips inside easily, his thick shaft sheathed inside me, filling me again to the brim. I'll never be this...full again. This crammed with Edward.

"No." I surge forward, wind my arms around his neck, push up and fit my lips to his. I open my mouth over his, and maybe I take him by surprise, for he parts his lips. I thrust my tongue inside his mouth, suck from him, draw from that minty darkness, inhale that cut grass scent that is so very Edward.

His big body shudders, then he kisses me back. Of course, Edward takes control of the kiss. He angles his head, deepens the kiss. Pushes me back into the mattress, swipes his tongue across my teeth, drags it along the inner seam of my lower lip. He plunders my mouth like it's his last kiss, his last time that he's going to be this close and... *No, no, no. I can't let him go.* No matter that he's trying to make me hate him. As efforts go, it's pathetic. If he thinks he can simply say and do things in the hope that it's going to make me dislike him, he is so wrong. I cling to him as he pushes forward and thrusts into me. As he impales me over and over again. As he pistons his hips forward and rams into me with such force that both our bodies jolt with the action. As he hits that spot again deep inside me and the climax shudders out from the point of contact, races up my back, my neck.

He tears his mouth from mine and whispers, "Come."

And I burst into flames as he roars above me and empties himself inside of me.

He stays poised above me for a few seconds more, sharing my breath, his lips a hair's breadth away from mine, his eyes open and holding mine, as if he can't bear to shut them.

I hold his gaze, tracing the webwork of fine lines that radiate from the edges of his eyes. The thick hair that falls across his brow. The ridiculously long eyelashes that fan out above his cheeks. The patrician nose, the stern upper lip, that pouty lower lip, that I want to kiss. I draw my finger down the scar on his cheek, then tip my chin up. I raise my mouth to his and he moves away.

He releases his hold under my knees, pulls out of me, then rolls over the side of the bed. He turns to walk into the bathroom and I take in the marks on his back. What the—? Did someone whip him? Did he whip himself? And not too long ago, by the looks of it.

He comes back with a wet towel that he uses to wipe between my legs. He tosses the cloth aside, then turns to leave, when I jump up and throw myself at him. "Edward, don't go."

He stays silent.

"Please, just hold me. I need you, Ed. Please."

He draws in a breath and his shoulders shudder. Then he turns. He pushes me back onto the bed. He pulls the covers up over me. I am about to protest when he slips in next to me. He presses down on my shoulder indicating that I should turn over, and when I do, he winds his arm around my waist and pulls me to him. I weave my fingers with his where they rest on my belly. His hand is so big that his palm covers the expanse of my stomach. My back is pressed into his chest; his half-erect dick settles in the valley between my arse-cheeks. His thighs cradle the backs of mine; his knees lock into the grooves behind mine.

His warmth envelops me. His scent is all around me. And I know I should turn around to face him, throw my arms around him and hold him close and tell him not to leave me, because I know he's going to.

As soon as I close my eyes, he'll be gone, and I'll never see him again. I half turn, when he slides his arm under my neck, curls that big forearm above my breasts. He tucks my head under his chin and orders, "Get some sleep."

I shouldn't. I should ask him what happened that had him come to me and simultaneously decide to leave me. I want to tell him I didn't tell him I was a virgin because I wanted him to be the first. My first. That there will never be anyone else. Instead, my eyelids flutter down and darkness drags me under, but I resist it.

Instead, I mumble, "Ed?"

"Hmm?"

"I saw the lash streaks on your back."

He stiffens, but doesn't say anything.

"Do you whip yourself, Ed?" I bite down on my lower lip. "Is that how you punish yourself? Is this how you deal with the aftermath of the incident?"

Tension radiates off of him and his big body seems to grow even more tense. Then he blows out a breath, "Sleep Ava, close your eyes."

*I can't. I don't want to. If I do, you'll leave and I don't want that. I don't want you to leave.*

"Ed," I swallow, "don't go, please."

"I have to, Eve."

"I can't live without you."

"You can."

"No," I whine, "I'll die if you go."

"You'll regret it if I stay."

"It's not true," I insist. "You know it isn't."

"So far, I've done what was best for me, but from now on, everything I do, I do for you."

"That sounds like a bad Bryan Adams song."

He chuckles, the sound without humor. "That's me, one bad pun after the other, baby."

"I love it when you call me baby." I yawn so widely that my jaw cracks.

"Sleep, baby." He presses his lips to the top of my head. This time sleep envelops me.

I come awake with a start, knowing something is wrong. I turn on my back to find I am alone in bed. Pale light filters in through the crack between the curtains. I spring up, throw off the cover, swing my legs over the bed, and race into the living room to find his backpack gone. I run back into the ensuite bathroom and his clothes are gone. Shit, shit shit. I knew I shouldn't have slept. Knew he'd leave. Knew he'd take off, and now I'll never see him again. *No, don't even go there. You're going to find him, wherever he is.*

I am not going to let him walk away from me like this. I round the bed, stare at the nightstand next to where he'd slept. Nothing. What had I been expecting? A note? What would he say? "Thank you for offering me your arse and your pussy and your mouth, but no thank you. It isn't enough."

What had last night been all about, anyway? He'd walked in, filled with purpose, then seemed to lose himself somewhere in between. He'd shown he could be caring and tender, only to do an about-face and be nasty to me, then seemed to turn passionate again. Shit. Something had been wrong. All those hidden messages in what he'd told me... I'd almost grasped them, then put them aside because I'd been too focused on what he'd been doing to my body. Oh, he'd made sure to distract me alright, and I'd fallen for it. If he had known I was a virgin, he wouldn't even have come to me, right? So, I should be grateful he had...but then he had left me. Bloody hell, what am I going to do now?

The sound of a bike revving reaches me. What the—? Has he been outside all this time? Has he been waiting for me to go out to him? Have I missed my chance to stop him? I race to my closet, pull on a dress, then run into the living room. I grab my house keys from the table near the entrance, then shove open the front door, run down the steps, over the short garden path and onto the road, just in time to see him round the corner on the bike.

"Edward," I scream and give chase. My bare feet thud against the sidewalk. The impact of each step ricochets through me as I race forward. I reach the bend, turn, my feet stumble over a crack in the pavement. The ground comes up to meet me. I close my eyes, brace for impact, only to be hauled up and against something hard.

"Watch where you are going," a rough voice rumbles. The vibrations shiver over the planes of the chest against which I am pressed.

My heart leaps in my chest and my belly trembles. "Edward." My lips widen in a smile. "You didn't leave. Oh, Edward! I knew you wouldn't go." I tilt my head up. "I knew you wouldn't—" My gaze clashes with unfamiliar blue eyes. So cold, so chilling. Eyes so dead that, surely, the soul behind them belongs to someone who's seen too much, who has no humanity left in him. Eyes which are the exact opposite of Edward's smoldering golden ones.

"Y... you?" I stutter. "Who're you?"

"Baron." His jaw tics. "I'm Baron, and you're in my way."

To find out what happens next read *Billionaire's Promise* HERE

Read an Excerpt


Ava


Baron? I blink, why is that name so familiar? "Do I know you?" I scowl, "And what do you mean that I am in your way? I almost fell—"

"Until you didn't," he points out. "I saved you from hurting yourself."

"I thought you were someone else." I take in his harsh features, the dark blonde hair that falls over his forehead, the rich tan of his skin which hints at a life spent outdoors, the dark eyelashes that fringe a pair of brilliant blue eyes. The kind of eyes you could drown in, get lost in. So deep that they hide secrets. Secrets which I have had enough of. I no longer want to be drawn into something I can't fathom. I yank at his grasp and he releases me so suddenly that I stumble back. He grips my shoulder, holds me long enough to ensure that I've found my balance, then releases me.

"You're better off without him." His lips twist.

"How do you know that?" A chill runs up my spine and I wrap my arms around myself.

"Anyone who has you running barefoot on the sidewalk at," he glances at the watch on his thick wrist, "six in the morning, clearly doesn't deserve you."

"And I suppose you do?" I purse my lips together. What the hell is wrong with me? Why am I baiting him? Why does he rub me the wrong way, and after he'd saved me from a bad fall? I could have hurt myself... Not that I could be hurt any worse, after how Edward had turned and left.

Edward. I swing around and stare at the now deserted road. The houses on either side of the quiet London street mock me. The fog that envelops the street clears, and for a second, I think I see him in the distance. I take a step forward, trip over the same crack in the pavement. Damn it! I stumble once more and when thick fingers wrap themselves around my wrist, I try to shake them off. "Let go of me," I huff.

"Why should I when, clearly, you can't put one foot in front of the other without hurting yourself?"

"You're hurting me now." I glance down at where his massive palm is curled around my hand. Warm tanned skin, scarred knuckles that lead up to a veined forearm, peppered with hair. The sheer masculinity of this man is overwhelming. I glance up again into those blue eyes. The scowl that laces his features, the grooves etched into his forehead hinting at his permanent dark mood.

He releases me, and I turn back toward the image I'd seen, but the road is empty. The early morning sun's rays slant down, and the fog seems to disperse in front of my eyes.

"He's gone," I mumble. "I couldn't stop him." A tear squeezes out from the corner of my eye and I slap it away angrily.

"No one's worth crying over."

"Oh?" I swallow down the ball of emotion that clogs my throat, then pivot and brush past him. "And how would you know that?"

"Because I spent a lot of my early years crying over something that could never be righted."

"You?" I pause, then stare at him across my shoulder. I tilt my head up, all the way up, to take in his massive height. He's as tall as Edward... No, taller. And his shoulders are broader. His massive chest hints at hours spent in some kind of physical work. Maybe he trains a lot? Or he's in some kind of profession that demands he stay in top condition? What do I care anyway? Edward is gone. He hadn't left behind even a note. He'd shagged me—okay, so I'd asked him to shag me, fine, not denying that—and then he'd left.

He'd crept away while I was asleep, after promising we'd be together, and now I am never going to see him again. My stomach twists, my guts churn, and the bile rolls up my throat. Goddam it. I spring to the side, fall to my knees, and am violently sick. I retch so hard, tears run from my eyes again, my hair falls over my face, and then he's there. He piles my hair on top of my head, holds my forehead while I empty my guts out. Somebody, kill me. This has to be the worst day of my life. Getting sick, and because that's not bad enough, in front of a stranger.

When I am done, he offers me his handkerchief. I glance up at him, and he jerks his chin, "Take it."

When I don't reach for it, he pats my mouth with the fabric. I snatch it from him, turn my face away and dab at my lips. I rise up, and he's with me. I turn and am about to hand the cloth back to him, then grimace and stuff it in the back pocket of my jeans. "I'll wash it and give it back to you."

I turn away, take a step forward and my legs seem to turn to jelly. Fuck me, what the hell is wrong with me? The ground comes up to meet me again, and this time, I am not surprised when he scoops me up.

"Put me down," I mumble.

He doesn't reply. Instead, he begins to walk back the way I'd come. "Which house?" he asks, his tone brusque.

"That one." I point toward the first house on our right.

He walks toward it, up the garden path, then takes the stairs two at a time, as if he isn't carrying me. Not that I weigh much, but hey, he could, at least, be out of breath or something. But there's not a hitch or any change in his breathing pattern to indicate that he is carrying the weight of another person. He stops at my front door.

I reach into my front pocket, pull out my keys. He shifts my weight, takes the key from me, unlocks the door, then walks through, before crossing the floor to the settee where he deposits me. He straightens then points a finger at me. "Stay there."

"Not that I was going anywhere, but seriously, what the hell is your problem?" I huff. "And I didn't give you permission to come into my house." I frown.

He arches an eyebrow, trains those piercing blue eyes on me, and I subside.

He places the keys on the coffee table then pivots and walks toward my kitchen as if he owns the place. Shit, the way his massive frame takes up space, he does, actually. His physical presence seems to absorb all of the oxygen in the space and my lungs burn.

Or maybe that's because of the growing realization that I've lost him. I've lost Edward. Had I ever had him? And he never told me that he isn't returning, but the sick sensation at the bottom of my stomach insists that he won't be anytime soon. My palms sweat and my chest hurts. I sit up and the world swims around me again.

"I told you to stay put," he chides as he appears from the direction of the kitchen. He squats down in front of me, handing me a glass of water.

I take it and drink from it, upturn the glass, but he grips my wrist. "Not too much or it'll make you sick again."

I lower it, glance through my eyelashes at him. He takes the glass from me, places it on the table.

"How are you feeling now?" He searches my face.

"Better," I mutter. "I need to brush my teeth."

He peruses my features then nods, rises to his feet, and scoops me up with him.

"I can walk," I protest.

He simply stalks into the bedroom, putting me down at the entrance to the bath.

I step inside, turn to shut the door to find him standing, hands folded, a stillness about him that is at odds with just how alert his eyes are.

"You can go," I mumble, "I'll be fine."

He doesn't move. Not so much as blinks an eye.

"Whatever." I sigh, then close the door and lock it. Not that I don't trust him. Okay, I don't trust him. So what if he saved me from hurting myself, then hauled me back in here and made sure I was hydrated? I'd trusted Edward and what did he do...? He broke his vows for me. He fucked me. OMG, he took my virginity and then left me. He's not coming back, and once more, I've screwed up my life.

I had gone after the impossible. He'd been a priest, for hell's sake. Why did I have to fall for him? Why had I been so attracted to him that I couldn't conceivably want anyone else but him? Of course. Not only had I spoiled my career by leaving behind the safety of a degree and a possible nine-to-five job, but then I also had to go after a completely unsuitable man. Typical Eve.

Eve. Now I'm calling myself Eve? My heart seems to shatter. I crumple to the floor, hide my face in my hands and begin to weep. Large sobs that hurt my chest, fill my throat, and overflow until I am sure I am going to shatter into a million pieces, and every one of them would still cry, Edward. Get over the dramarama, bitch. Clearly, I've been reading too many romance novels if I am becoming so over-the-top sentimental. But damn him, he broke my heart.

In such a short period of time, he'd crawled under my skin, and imprinted himself into my soul in a way... A way that only a man of God could have. Someone who was in service of a higher purpose than himself. Shit, what am I thinking? Why am I making excuses for him, when all he's done since I met him is give me second place in his life? He may have broken his vows for me, but then he left, and I simply cannot fathom why. Hell, maybe it wasn't even for me that he broke his vows. I may not know what happened, but clearly, there was something bothering him when he got here.

More tears well up and my pulse thuds at my temples. A banging sound fills my head and I am sure it is my heart pounding in my ears, but then a male voice calls behind me, "Open up, or I swear, I am going to break down this door."

"Shit. Shit. Shit. Shit." I scramble up, grab hold of a hand towel and wipe my face with it.

The banging increases in urgency, then the sound of a shoulder crashing against the bathroom door reaches me.

"Stop," I yelp as I rush toward it. The last thing I need is for the door to be broken down. The bloody landlord would definitely take it out of my deposit. I reach the doorway, yank it open and come face to face with Mr. Grumpy Pants himself.

"What's your problem?" I snap.

"You," he looks me up and down, "you're my problem."

"Jesus." I gape at him. "You insult me in my own home? If you hadn't helped me earlier—which, by the way, wasn't required. I can take care of myself, but you did and I am grateful for it, but now you can leave."

"No."

"What?"

"I'm not going anywhere," he informs me. "Not until you have a shower and get a good breakfast. You need it after your crying jag."

"Crying jag." I flush. Of course, he heard me weeping my stupid heart out. Why the hell does he care how I feel? Why is he so concerned about me? "Who the hell are you anyway?" I scowl. "You're seriously giving me the creeps, the way you've barged into my life."

"And you are getting antsy for no reason." He holds up his arms. "You can pat me down if you want. You'll see I'm not dangerous."

Dangerous? He doesn't need weapons to be dangerous.

I look him up and down. "No, thank you, and by the way, I am taken."

"Taken?"

I nod. "My uh...man... He just left earlier."

"That's who you were chasing after?"

"Only because he forgot his phone," I lie.

"He forgot his phone..." he says slowly.

"Y...yeah." I swallow.

"So, you were chasing after him, barefooted?"

I nod.

"So, where's his phone?"

"None of your business." I scowl. "Will you please step away now so I can shower?"

"Not stopping you."

Anger twists my guts and it feels good. Good to be able to focus on something else, other than that jerk-hole who walked out of my life. How dare he play with me like this? How dare he stalk in here, claim me, imprint himself all over me, then walk out without looking back once? How dare he?

I fist my hands at my sides, then step back and slam the door shut. I lock it again, march over to the shower and turn it on. I shed my clothes, step under the hot water and allow it to flow over me. A few hours ago, he'd stood here as I had sucked him off. Hell. Hell. Hell. No need to figure out if I will be going to hell for having teased the Father into breaking his vows... Clearly, I am already there.

Is this my punishment from the other One in our relationship? The One Above. The Almighty who, no doubt, is displeased with me for having tempted one of His own to sin. Gah, stop that. Why are you questioning things as if the Father's influence has rubbed off on you? Not long ago, he'd been here rubbing off on me. Ugh. Stop that. He's gone, remember?

He left you.

Walked out without a backward glance. So why are you still so... so...hung up on him?

I raise my head toward the spray, let the hot water wash away the tears. I stand under the pelting drops until my head clears somewhat. Then switch it off and dry myself. I wrap the towel around myself, secure it and walk into the bedroom. It's empty. Of course, it would be. Why had I thought otherwise? I walk over to my closet, pull on my underclothes, a pair of leggings and a sweatshirt.

I need to stop holding onto hope that he'll return to me. There's no reason to think he will. His actions had all been intended to hurt. Clearly, he wants me to forget about him. Except, he took my virginity, something I'll never forget. To be fair, I hadn't mentioned to him that I was a virgin. Thank God for that. I got to spend some time with him. Yeah, and he broke your heart too, how about that, hmm?

It's only your heart... It will mend... Unlike whatever he is facing. It has to be something catastrophic that propelled Edward to leave behind the priesthood and take off. Something I intend to get to the bottom of.

I grab a hair tie, pile my hair on top of my head, then walk out of the bedroom, across the living room toward the kitchen.

The scent of toast and coffee reaches me. My stomach growls. I step inside the kitchen, pause. His back is to me and his broad shoulders are framed against the first rays of the sun that pour in. They halo him, highlight him, make him seem larger than life. A behemoth. Someone who came into my life, for what? To save me? From Edward? From myself? A shiver runs down my spine. I shake my head, walk over to the coffee pot to pour myself a cup. He turns to me then. "Sit." He jerks his head toward the table. "I'll pour it for you."

"But—"

"Go on," he says, his voice impatient. "This will go much faster if you cooperate."

I blink. "Excuse me?"

"I mean," he schools his features into an expression of patience, "sit down, please."

I hesitate. That please? It didn't sound like he meant it. In fact, it sounded as if he'd said it with much reluctance. He raises an eyebrow, turns his gaze to the table then back at me.

Fine, be like that. I slap the mug back on the kitchen counter, stomp over to the table and seat myself. I play with the ends of my hair, pull off the band and place it on the table. Then drum my fingers on the table. He turns, surveys my restless fingers, and I cease the movement instantly. Goosebumps flare on my skin. What is it about his glare that makes me want to rush to obey him?

He pours me a cup of coffee, brings it over, along with a stack of pancakes on a plate. On a second plate he's piled hash browns, baked beans and toast, which he places between us.

I blink down at the two plates, then up at him. "Uh, who is all this for?"

"You." He turns to grab his own plate, then sits opposite me. "I substituted flaxseeds for the eggs for the pancakes," he remarks.

I glance at him. "You did?"

He nods.

"How do you know that I am vegetarian?"

"Because you don't keep any meat or fish or eggs at home?"

Right. "I do eat milk and eggs," I mutter. "Just happen to be out of them..." I shuffle my feet, "the eggs, I mean." Gah, shut up, what's wrong with me? Why do I tend to babble in his presence? Why does he make me nervous?

He picks up his fork and knife, then eyes me across the table. "You're not eating," he admonishes.

"Neither are you."

His lips quirk, then he glances down and digs into his food.

I follow his lead, manage to make my way through a quarter of the pancakes, before I give up and lean back. I watch him demolish the food on his plate like he hasn't eaten in years.

When he glances up, I push my half-filled plate toward him.

He scowls at it. "You haven't eaten nearly enough."

"It's enough," I insist.

"It's enough when I say it is."

I blink at him, "Seriously, you didn't just say that."

"What's wrong with what I said?"

"Are you trying to be funny or something?"

"I've never been more serious." He leans forward, "You need your energy; you are wasting away."

I scoff. "I wouldn't call this," I point at myself, "wasting away."

"You're right."

"I am?"

He nods. "You have decent curves. I've seen better, of course, but you'll do."

I gape at him. "You...you're...something, you know that?"

"I often have that effect on women."

I jump to my feet. "Out. Get out."

He meets my gaze with a cool glance. "You're overreacting."

"And you're not welcome here anymore."

"I'm afraid that's not your call to make."

"What?" I frown. "This is my apartment and you are seated at my table—"

"In front of a breakfast I cooked for you."

"A breakfast you can shove up your—"

He tilts his head, and there's just enough warning in that single glance for me to press my lips together. Why the hell had I allowed him, a complete stranger, into my home? And yet, why does that jut of his jaw, the spark of anger in his eyes, feel so...right?

No, no, no. This can't be happening. I just had one man walk out on me a few hours ago, and already, I am attracted to another? Talk about being a slut. Only I'm not one. Hell, I'd never wanted to sleep with anyone else before Edward. And now, suddenly, here's another man, someone to whom I am attracted just as much? With as much intensity as Ed... It's the same... Yet different, though. With Ed...the pull had been sharp, incisive, almost clinical in the precision with which my heart had gravitated toward him. Probably because once I'd realized that he was a priest, every single interaction with him had felt wrong...but with Baron...there's a freedom. A need... An overwhelming pull to throw myself at him, throw myself at his mercy, and beg him to do anything he wants with me. Maybe the need Edward ignited opened up a hotbed of something... Some nameless emotion, some twisting sensation that I had hidden away for too long. And now it's out there, and I feel like I am exposed and aching and throbbing and crying out for attention.

My chest tightens. My scalp tingles. My skin suddenly feels too tight for my body. I take a breath and my lungs burn. My knees knock together and I sit down in the chair so suddenly that the legs creak.

"You okay?" His gaze intensifies as he peruses my features and I look away.

Heat flushes my skin and my toes curl. My own thoughts have aroused me in a way that I never would have expected. My thighs clench and my center throbs. The soreness in my backside and between my legs pulses and writhes. Shit, what's wrong with me? I place my elbows on the table, bury my face in my hands.

I sense him move then. Hear his chair scrape as he pushes it back. The pad of his footsteps, the sound of a glass being filled with water. His footsteps approach, then I hear the thunk of the glass hitting the table in front of me.

"Drink," he commands.

I stiffen. What the hell is his problem?

"Do it," he insists.

I lower my hands and scowl at him.

He simply folds his arms across his chest and glares at me.

Jerk.

I glower back, and his gaze simply intensifies. Hot, burning, overwhelming. The flesh between my legs throbs. Heat flushes my cheeks. I glance away, take a sip. And does the man move away? Of course, not. He waits until I tilt the glass and drink half its contents.

Satisfied, he sits down, pushes my untouched coffee mug toward me.

I reach for it, take a sip. The bitter taste of the java blooms on my palate. I sigh out my appreciation, take another sip. Dark, rich notes of chocolate, laced with a sweeter taste of honey, and in between, the characteristic bitterness of coffee flickers across my tongue. "It's good." I blink up at him. "Which coffee grinds did you use?"

"The one you had in your coffee canister?"

"Oh." I glance down at the cup, take another sip. "You sure?"

"Yeah."

There's an amused edge to his tone. I glance up to find his lips twitch.

"No need to make a national joke out of my question," I mutter. "It's simply that the coffee tastes so much better than when I make it."

"It happens." He raises his shoulders. "When someone else cooks the same dish you do, they have a different touch, a unique way of assembling the ingredients, which will, therefore, be perceived differently by your taste receptors."

"Oh." I blink. "Are you a chef?"

His features close. "No."

He gets up, takes both our plates and the used cutlery over to the sink and begins to wash up.

"I can do—"

He glares at me over his shoulder, and I shut up. Of course, Mr. Growly Pants will do what he wants, when he wants. He finishes the washing up—returns for my now empty coffee cup—which he takes to the sink along with his, and washes that up too. He finishes drying them, puts them away—in the correct places on the shelves, then wipes the counter clean.

"Make yourself at home," I bite out. "In fact, why don't you move in, while you're at it?"

He pauses, then turns to me. "Not yet."

My jaw drops. "What do you mean, not yet? I don't know you at all. You're a complete stranger and—"

"My point exactly." He folds his arms across his impressive chest and his T-shirt stretches across those beautifully sculpted pecs. His biceps bulge, drawing my attention to his thick veiny forearms.

My throat dries. My tongue seems to be stuck to the roof of my mouth. All the moisture in my body has drained to that single pulsing point between my legs. I gulp. "What..." I clear my throat, "What are you trying to say?"

"That you are too innocent."

I laugh, "Trust me, if you knew what I've been up to, you wouldn't say that."

His gaze narrows and color smears his cheeks. He opens his mouth, then closes it again. "What you have done or not done in the past is none of my business."

"Oh?"

He jerks his chin. "I am more concerned with the now, the present. The fact that you let me, a complete stranger, into your flat."

"You know what?" I scowl at him. "It's time you left."

"Oh, believe me, I am. I have no intention of staying, now that I know you are safe."

"The only threat here is from you."

"As I was saying..." he enunciates each word slowly, "you...allowed...me—someone you don't know— into your flat."

"You helped me earlier," I point out.

"I could have been simply trying to gain your trust."

"Is that what you were trying to do?"

"No." He blows out a breath. "I was trying to stop you from hurting yourself."

"So, you're not a stranger anymore."

"I was when you met me."

"Everyone's a stranger when you first meet them!" I throw up my hands. "You caught me at a weak moment, okay? And this back and forth is making my head spin. What's your point anyway?"

"That you shouldn't let anyone you don't know inside your home."

And sometimes, you shouldn't let even those you think you do know, because actually you don't...you don't know them at all. Damn you, Edward. I squeeze my eyes shut. "You are right. I'll be more careful next time."

"Good."

I open my eyelids to find him walking out of the kitchen. I reach for my hair band, find it's gone. Huh? I could swear I placed it on the table earlier. I shake my head, then rise to my feet and follow him. He snatches up the jacket he'd abandoned at some point on the arm of the couch; shrugs into it, then walks to the front door, opens it.

"Wait," I burst out. He pauses, turns to me. Waits as I try to figure out exactly what it is I want to tell him. What do I want from him? Why do I want anything from him? He's a stranger, right? So why doesn't he feel that way? Why do I feel like I already know him at some level? A wave of tiredness washes over me. I curl my fingers around the frame of the kitchen doorway where I am poised. "My name is Ava, Ava Erikson."

"I know."

"You do?"

He nods, then points to where I've placed my mail on the table near the doorway.

"Right."

He turns away, when I stop him again. "Wait." I call out to him and he stops, "Will I see you again?" I ask.

He hesitates then glances at me over his shoulder. "Do you want to see me again, Ava?"

*To find out what happens next get Billionaire's Promise HERE*

BINGE READ THE BIG BAD BILLIONAIRE SERIES
US
UK
ALL MARKETS
START THE SERIES WITH SINCLAIR & SUMMER'S STORY HERE

Read Saint & Victoria's story here

Read Weston & Amelie's story here

Read Damian & Julia's story here

Join my newsletter

Claim your *FREE* contemporary romance book. Click *HERE*

Claim your *FREE* paranormal romance book *HERE*

Follow me on AMAZON

Follow me on BookBub

Follow on Goodreads

Follow me on TikTok

Follow my Pinterest boards

Follow me on FB

Follow me on Instagram

Join my secret Facebook Reader Group; I am dying to meet YOU!

Read my Books HERE

# FREE BOOKS

❀ Created with Vellum

Made in the USA
Monee, IL
22 March 2024

55341956R00121